"All I'm trying to tell you
is that I don't think
we can work together—
on a climb or
anything else," Susan said.

"No?" It was a single, softly spoken word, but it carried a depth and breadth of meaning Susan couldn't begin to decipher.

"I think you'd better leave," she said in a strangled voice. "I think—"

"Let me tell you what *I* think," Jack said purposefully. His hand shot out and circled her wrist, pulling her insistently toward him. He leaned down toward her, cupping her face in his hands, his fingers splaying through the disarrayed locks of her hair. "I think I'm just going to have to spend the night."

She opened her mouth to protest just as his head swooped down to hers. Much to her surprise, instead of issuing a passionate refusal, she found herself accepting the salty probing of his tongue...

Dear Reader:

Summer is here! And we've got six new SECOND CHANCE AT LOVE romances to add to your pleasure in the new season. So sit back, put your feet up, and enjoy . . .

You've also got a lot to look forward to in the months ahead—delightful romances from exciting new writers, as well as fabulous stories from your tried-and-true favorites. You know you can rely on SECOND CHANCE AT LOVE to provide the kind of satisfying romantic entertainment you expect.

We continue to receive and enjoy your letters—so please keep them coming! Remember: Your thoughts and feelings about SECOND CHANCE AT LOVE books are what enable us to publish the kind of romances you not only enjoy reading once, but also keep in a special place and read again and again.

Warm wishes for a beautiful summer,

Ellen Edwards

Ellen Edwards
SECOND CHANCE AT LOVE
The Berkley Publishing Group
200 Madison Avenue
New York, N.Y. 10016

Second Chance at Love

HEAD OVER HEELS

NICOLA ANDREWS

**A
SECOND CHANCE AT LOVE
BOOK**

Other Second Chance at Love books by
Nicola Andrews

FORBIDDEN MELODY   #139
RECKLESS DESIRE   #180

HEAD OVER HEELS

First edition published June 1984

First printing

"Second Chance at Love" and the butterfly emblem are trademarks
belonging to Jove Publications, Inc.

Printed in the United States of America

Second Chance at Love books are published by
The Berkley Publishing Group
200 Madison Avenue, New York, NY 10016

To Mary Agnes DeA.

Chapter 1

IT WAS AT least a full minute before Susan Reed believed what she was seeing. First she had to correct for her angle of vision. Then she had to calculate. Then she had to make sure she hadn't made a mistake.

She hadn't. The man was huge. That she was so far below him and looking up had nothing to do with it. He had to be well over six feet tall. His shoulders weren't broad; they were massive. Susan wondered if he had trouble finding shirts to fit him. And jeans! Hadn't she heard somewhere that the longest jeans you could buy had a thirty-eight-inch inseam? This man's legs had to be longer than that. They seemed to go on forever, their muscled contours straining against the denim.

There was a short, sharp gust of wind. Susan forced her body to relax. She had to be crazy. Here she was, hanging by a rope from a stationary piton, swinging in the air seven hundred feet above a heap of jagged, barren rocks, worrying about where some strange man bought his clothes.

Not that she was really in any danger. The first dizzying drop was over. The piton had held, and so had her safety rope. From here on in it was strictly a procedural problem. The man on the ledge above her couldn't know that, however. He couldn't tell by looking at her that she was an experienced Alpine climber who'd been in this situation before and knew what to do about it. All he could see was a five-feet-three, one-hundred-and-ten-pound redhead hanging from an outcrop a quarter of the way up one of the most difficult ascents in Switzerland.

The wind died. Susan stiffened, rocked, and swung herself up. She grabbed the rope and held on, glad to be vertical again. The man had come to help, and she wasn't going to object to that at this point. She just hoped she'd have the presence of mind to conduct a polite conversation once she met him.

She hadn't had too many polite conversations with the breed of male known as the Alpine Mountain Climber. The men who came to Switzerland to conquer the Alps tended to be extremely negative about women climbers. Women were cowardly, they said. Women were timid. Women had no sense of balance or natural coordination.

It was useless to throw out counterexamples. Exceptions just proved the rule.

Susan's father had taught her to climb in Wyoming's Grand Tetons, where women had been more readily accepted in the climbing community. Her first year in the Alps had come as a bad shock. To get a reputation for being as good as a man, you had to be better than all but a tiny group of Master Climbers, who outshone everyone. To escape the charge of cowardice, you had to take chances no man would ever consider. And you had to prove yourself over and over and over again.

But not now, Susan told herself firmly. What she had

to do now was get herself back to that ledge.

"Are you anchored?" The voice drifted down to her, deep, but faint and misty.

Susan held more tightly to the rope and bellowed back, "I'm fine. Do you know how to haul me up?" She mentally crossed her fingers, hoping the man wouldn't say yes if he didn't. If he bounced her against the ledge a few times, she'd be black and blue and sore for a week, and she had classes to teach.

"Where's your hat?"

Susan's right hand automatically went to her head. All she felt was thick red hair knotted into braids. Damn. No wonder her ears were freezing. Her hat must have fallen when she did.

She leaned back and called out again, "Do you know how to haul me up?"

She thought she saw the man nod, but she wasn't sure. She'd give him a few minutes, she decided, and if she didn't feel a tug on the rope she'd start swinging. Doing it by herself would be the hard way, but it would be preferable to being hauled up by an amateur.

There was a tug on the rope, and Susan held her breath. She was swinging, steadying, swinging again. He was not, however, trying to haul her up *while* she was swinging. He waited until the rope hung straight, hauled up a few inches until it started to sway, then waited until it was straight again.

She sighed with relief and spent the time in reflection. In the three years since she had settled in Bresson, Switzerland, she had made most of the training climbs in the vicinity by herself, and a few of the Intermediate-Difficulty and Basic climbs with her students. She hadn't, however, been able to manage a professional, Extreme-Difficulty climb herself.

She'd scarcely even realized how much she'd missed serious climbing. There had been such a lot to do: establishing the Women's Alpine Climbing School, developing routines for the students who came from as far away as California to train, learning how to keep books and decipher tax forms in German. The time had just slipped by, and since she was living among her beloved Alps, she had thought she was happy.

She was certainly happier than she had been back in Wyoming, fighting with nice, staid Dan about whether or not a *real* woman would do something as dangerous as mountain climbing. Dan's problem was that he didn't think even men should do anything as dangerous as mountain climbing. Dan's three gods were safety, security, and predictability. He couldn't conceive of the idea that some people might find safety dull and danger a necessary spice in life.

She wasn't going to think about Dan, she reminded herself, relaxing against the rope as the man at the other end of it inched her up past the concave hollow in the mountain. Her marriage to Dan was long past. He had hurt her terribly, but it was over. She concentrated on her climbing now.

Or, she told herself, she *should* concentrate on her climbing. Maybe it was time to look for a major expedition to join, or time to organize one herself. She had almost forgotten what a wonderful feeling it was to be in the Alps with people who knew mountains and how to climb them. It was looking danger in the face and knowing you could beat it, knowing you could get up and down again safely—that was the thrill. When that happened, you owned that mountain, and you could never lose it again. Which, Susan thought wryly, beat affairs of the heart by a country mile.

She saw the ledge shelf above her and reached out to grab it. Almost home free.

The man was even more impressive up close than he had been from the end of the rope. He positively loomed above her, making her feel incredibly tiny. That he was startlingly handsome didn't make him easier to look at calmly, either. Susan didn't think she'd ever met anyone with such sheer animal magnetism, such commanding sexual presence. Just looking at him made her wonder what it would be like to feel his hands in her hair, his lips against her throat, his strong arms crushing her shoulders to his chest . . .

She blushed furiously, deciding she must be getting altitude sickness. She didn't even know the man's name. Dan might have been a long time ago, and there had been no one since, but that was no reason to start having lewd fantasies about a perfect stranger.

She stuck out her hand, hoping to cover her confusion. "I'm Susan Reed," she told him, wanting to kick herself for sounding so breathless.

"Jack Cameron." He took her hand. In some deep well of absolute consciousness, Susan noticed that he managed to sound both angry and amused at once. She in turn felt as if she'd been hit on the head with a brick. Jack Cameron, she thought wildly, trying to stifle an insane desire to laugh. She couldn't get picked up by some passing climber. She had to be rescued by Jack Cameron. If she were a mathematician who'd just made a stupid mess of a simple equation, she'd probably get bailed out by Einstein.

Maybe it wasn't the same Jack Cameron. She dismissed the thought as soon as she had it. The man was too at ease with the mountains, too at ease with his own body, to be anyone else. She should have guessed he was a master climber the moment she looked at him.

She slipped her nylon day pack off her back and began plunging through it, looking for her spare hat. At least it was something she could do other than stare at the man. "I can get down by myself," she said hastily, pulling the hat out and cramming it over her ears. "If you want to go farther up, I mean. I— What's the matter?"

Susan was suddenly very conscious of the fact that he was staring at her, and she was staring back at him. Now that her gaze had rested on his features, it seemed impossible to tear it away. He had such an unusual face. Thick, straight blond hair the color of sweet corn topped straight eyebrows, wide dark eyes, a perfectly formed nose, high cheekbones, and a stubbornly square jaw. Darkly wind-tanned skin framed eyes so black there seemed to be no distinction between iris and pupil. Susan stared into them, fascinated. She'd read stories in which the romantic hero had so-called fathomless eyes, but she'd always thought the notion fanciful. Now she knew what the writers had been talking about. She could have stared into those eyes forever.

"It's the cap," Jack Cameron said. "I'm glad I don't have a complete amateur on my hands."

His words broke her concentration, and she was at once embarrassed and piqued. He was glad he didn't have a *complete* amateur on his hands, was he? Well, she wasn't any kind of amateur at all. She had a better ascent record than ninety percent of the men in the Alps. If she had any sense she'd—

Calm down, she told herself fiercely. This was Jack Cameron, one of the most famous master climbers in the history of the sport. Next to him, she might as well be an amateur. Besides, he didn't know her or anything about her. All he knew was that he'd rescued her from an accident on a training climb he could have completed blindfolded.

But he didn't think she was competent. Susan was surprised at herself. What difference did it make if Jack Cameron thought she was competent or not? She didn't even know the man, and, considering the circles he frequented, she wasn't likely to get to know him. She'd walk away from this ledge and never see him again.

Still, the thought rankled. She hated that he was standing a few feet from her, thinking of her as . . . inept.

She started to pull her pack over her shoulders. If she was so interested in making a good impression, the best thing she could do was get out of here quickly and unobtrusively. That way she wouldn't ruin his afternoon the way she'd undoubtedly ruined his morning. She might even be able to calm herself down. The man was having a distinctly disturbing effect on her.

"Do you always climb this thing alone?"

Susan jumped, surprised to hear his resonant voice after so long a silence. Why did the man make her so nervous? She was usually very easygoing.

"I do the training climbs by myself," she told him. "I've probably done them all a couple of hundred times apiece. They're good exercise."

He looked surprised. "That's all you do?" he asked disbelievingly. "Make training climbs?"

Susan shook her head vigorously. "Not usually," she told him. "I used to climb regularly, but now, with my school, I don't have time to do much but intermediate climbs with students. I did do the Matterhorn about three years ago," she rushed on, anxious to avoid giving him the impression that she made only unimportant ascents.

"Did you really?" He was staring off into the distance,

frowning a little and rubbing his chin.

Susan wondered if she had been trying too hard to impress him. Probably. But there was nothing odd about wanting to impress one of the greatest practitioners of the sport she loved so much. Any mountain climber in the world would give both eyeteeth to impress Jack Cameron. She wished he wouldn't be so . . . distant.

"So you often climb alone?"

Susan blinked. Cameron's tone wasn't distant now. It was biting, sarcastic, cold, and there was a hard, almost accusing glare in his eyes. What had changed in that split second he'd spent looking into the distance?

She backed away from him, finding his size not only impressive but a little frightening as well. He seemed to fill up the landscape. Suddenly she wanted to be away from him, down the mountain, back in the safety of her battered little chalet.

"It isn't safe to climb alone," he said, sounding calmer now, patient. "You could get hurt. You almost did get hurt. Someday someone else is going to get hurt trying to save your neck."

Susan bristled. The patronizing reasonableness of his statements infuriated her. No matter who he was, he had no right to talk to her as if she were a child who'd been caught with her Sunday dress all muddy. She hated being patronized. She especially hated being lectured about safety. After two years with Dan—

Calm down, calm down, she instructed herself again. Take two deep breaths. She did so and was instantly aware of her lungs. They ached. She was freezing.

"Look," she said, "I'm grateful for your help, and I'm sorry I spoiled your climb. I won't spoil any more of it by keeping you out here talking. I have to get back to teach a class anyway, so if you don't mind—"

"Of course I mind," he interrupted irritably. "I don't

like the idea that you're climbing around out here by yourself. It's dangerous!"

"It's *not* dangerous!" Susan exploded. She'd had this conversation before. *Dangerous*. Dan's favorite word. "I'm an expert climber," she told him, "and I've made over two hundred ascents in the Alps. I've made this very climb more than fifty times. I know what I'm doing!"

"And you still had an accident," Cameron pointed out. "It could have been a bad accident."

"Which it wasn't," Susan retorted. "Because I know what I'm doing well enough to anchor myself to stationary pitons only after I've checked them, and to double-shank-knot my rope. I'm not some amateur who needs to be told the definition of a pull line!"

"Neither am I."

Jack Cameron's eyes were so steely, so coldly angry, she almost missed his words. Almost, but not quite. The man had a lot of nerve. Did he always try to ride roughshod over people this way? Did he think being designated a master climber gave him the right to unleash his self-righteous arrogance on anyone who happened along?

"No," she told him through clenched teeth. "Nobody thinks you're an amateur, Mr. Cameron. But please note that you *are* up on this mountain, and you *did* get here by yourself."

He started advancing on her, his jaw set, his eyes stormy. Susan took a few steps backward and stopped. She couldn't keep retreating; she didn't know how far she was from the ledge. Her heart was fluttering wildly, and her stomach was churning.

He stopped less than a foot away from her. Susan felt as if she was looking up at a skyscraper rather than a man—a huge, looming skyscraper that had suddenly come to handsome but menacing life. His mouth was set in an uncompromising line, the skin over his cheekbones pulled taut. Susan felt ready to melt into the ground.

"I came up here alone," he told her grimly, "because I followed you. I saw you set out alone, I knew you'd get into trouble, and I thought I'd be here to get you out of it. You did get into trouble, and I did get you out of it. You will therefore tie this line to your safety belt and follow me down." He dumped a hank of rope into her arms. "I have no intention of acting like a damn fool twice in one day."

I have no intention of acting like a damn fool twice in one day. If those words hadn't made Susan mad enough to spit, what happened in the course of the next half hour would have. Susan didn't think she'd ever been treated with such total contempt. Jack Cameron seemed determined to humiliate her in every possible way. He always took the higher—the lead or "safety"—position on the mountain. He never allowed himself to climb below her position line. When she stopped to rest, he climbed down until they were parallel, then waited until she once again began her descent.

Susan tried to tell herself this only made sense. After all, she wouldn't be able to catch and hold a two-hundred-pound man if she wanted to. But she couldn't make herself believe her own reasoning. Jack's behavior might have been appropriate on a major expedition, but on a training climb it was only courtesy to trade off the lead position with climbers whose abilities you respected. Jack Cameron might as well have been wearing a sandwich board announcing his utter lack of confidence in her expertise.

By the time she reached the third-last piton on the face, Susan's cheeks were numb with cold and her temper was ready to boil over. She had had just about all of

Jack Cameron she could take. If she put up with him much longer, she was going to do something really stupid. Stupid *and* dangerous, she amended to herself. And wouldn't he just love that.

She looked quickly up the mountain face. Jack was at least three pitons above her, his gaze turned upward. No doubt his studied indifference was just one more way of telling her how negligible he thought she was, but for the moment she didn't care. As long as he didn't realize what she was doing until she'd done it . . .

Quickly she threaded a yellow nylon rappel rope through the loops in her leather belt and anchored it to the piton. This was a zigzag pattern training climb, but that was only for the convenience of novice climbers who needed practice. Susan could see no serious reason not to rappel down the face. There were no sharp outcrops or gray patches of loose stones to stop her. Besides, rappeling was faster than zigzag descent. Instead of spending another fifteen minutes stoking her anger at Jack Cameron, she could be on the valley floor in less than three.

She untied the rope that linked her to Jack, then gave it three quick, vicious tugs to let him know she had severed their connection. A moment later she was bounding swiftly, freely down the sheer face of the mountain.

She hit ground before she'd really had a chance to feel the wind in her hair. There, she thought in satisfaction. That'll fix him. That'll—

She heard the sound above her before the first stones reached her feet. Appalled, she stared up at the figure leaping down and landing above her. She'd never seen anybody rappel that fast. If Jack's feet hadn't been loosening stones every time his boots slammed against the mountain face, Susan would have thought he was falling.

And he'd accused *her* of being reckless!

He was beside her almost before she realized it. And he was angry.

"What were you trying to do?" he demanded, grabbing her arm with such viciousness she could feel the steel of his fingers through all four layers of her clothing. "Don't you have any sense of responsibility at all? Don't you know a climber never leaves a member of his team alone on a face?"

Susan jerked away from him. "I wasn't going to leave you alone on the face," she told him hotly. "All I did was rappel down the slope. Quite frankly, Mr. Cameron, I'm tired of being accused of things I haven't done and had no intention of doing. And when I want instructions on how to climb—or descend—a mountain, I'll ask for them."

"Then you'd better start asking," Jack said grimly, "because if you continue to act this way, you're going to break your neck."

"Then if you don't mind, I'll go off somewhere and break it in peace," Susan shot back. "If I had a rock," she told Jack, "I'd break your head with it. Now that you're safely on the ground, of course."

Then she turned on her heel and walked away.

Chapter 2

BY THE TIME Susan reached the tiny, ramshackle chalet that housed both the Women's Alpine Climbing School and her own living quarters, some of her anger had dissipated. The distance she'd put between herself and that tantalizing, infuriating man had given her some perspective, and she'd come to the grudging conclusion that Jack Cameron had had a point. He had simply done what any expert climber would have done under the circumstances. She should have tried to reason with him, instead of lashing out. She should have behaved like an adult.

She stopped just outside the kitchen door, feeling the faint heat of a flush begin to spread across her face. *Behave like an adult*. That wasn't her phrase; it was Dan's. One of his favorites. Maybe that was why she'd reacted with such furious hostility to Jack Cameron. All that talk about danger. All that talk about safety. Susan could almost hear Dan's voice behind Jack Cameron's words.

She pounded into the kitchen, stripping off her gloves and throwing them onto the counter by the sink. She

13

wasn't going to think about Dan; she'd promised herself that. She hadn't even seen the man in three years. He was probably back in Wyoming, turning into a blubbering idiot every time his new wife passed another car on the right. If he let her drive at all.

Dan thought the world was a snake pit of disasters, and women totally incapable of handling it. His constant, worried carping had been destructive, undermining her confidence. Had he wanted her to end up a scared little rabbit who was afraid to poke her nose out of the house without his permission? Or was it possible that he had believed what he'd said to her about treacherous shoals and lurking monsters, that he honestly looked at the beauties of nature and the handiwork of humanity as nothing but a series of traps to be carefully avoided?

She shucked her blue nylon parka and hung it on a peg near the door, then started down the narrow hallway that led from the kitchen to the old pantry she had converted into an office. No more thinking about Dan, she vowed again. All these mental gymnastics did nothing to change what had happened between them, or what he had done to her in the end.

She made her way carefully through the stacks of unfiled papers and forms littering the office floor and wedged herself into the rickety wooden chair behind the ancient school desk she used for doing her paperwork. When she managed to do any paperwork, she chided herself. The office looked like a collection station for the Boy Scouts' annual paper drive. Ascent records, progress reports, tax forms, lesson plans—the piles were endless. When she had dreamed of settling in Switzerland and establishing an Alpine climbing school for women, it had never occurred to her that the project would generate so many pieces of paper in so many different languages. Not that she paid much attention to it...

Ignoring the thought that she was going to have to deal with it someday, she looked down at the messages Janie Dean, her newly hired assistant, had left for her. On the top was a wide piece of cardboard covered with four-inch-high block letters, as if Janie was taking no chances that Susan might miss it. CLAIRE HOLLOWAY'S, it read. TONIGHT AT SEVEN-THIRTY. YOU HAVE TO GO. *Have to go* was underlined three times.

Susan wrinkled her nose in distaste and put the cardboard aside. Claire Holloway was a rich, idle socialite who kept a twenty-room chalet halfway up the east, or nonascent, face of the Maidenhorn. Claire wanted to "know" climbing and climbers, which meant she wanted to entertain them. So during climbing season she threw lavish parties with guest lists drawn from the jet set and the world of international sports, and "everybody" went.

Susan hated the whole process. By the end of one of Claire's parties, Susan was ready to declare that all jet-setters were impossibly snobbish, all climbers impossibly stupid, and everybody impossibly drunk. She always came home after an evening at Claire's swearing she would never go again.

Unfortunately, this time Janie was right. She had to go. The Women's Alpine Climbing School was making its reputation by providing a workout unit for world-class women climbers, but it was making its money by teaching beginning mountain readiness to jet-set daughters whose parents had the wherewithal to fork out the stiff tuition fee for an eight-week course. All those parents would be at Claire's tonight, and they would expect Susan to be there, too, as part of their world.

She tossed the piece of cardboard onto the floor in disgust, decided she'd think about what to wear later, and went on to the other messages. The Société des Alpes had called, wanting to know her schedule for training climbs for the rest of the season. She didn't *have* a written schedule of training climbs. She never did. How could the Swiss expect one to be so organized? She made a note to Janie to send them something and tossed the message slip onto a pile of mountain weather forecasts.

The next message was from the mayor's office. She disposed of that one without reading it. If she had to do something for the mayor, Janie would tell her to do it.

The next message was from the Committee for a Safe Mountaineering Code, announcing the licensing panel meeting on the fourth. She checked her calendar. The fourth was, needless to say, Monday. Monday was her busiest day—four morning classes and three in the afternoon. The licensing panel meeting was for six, and if she made it at all, she'd probably fall asleep at the conference table.

She hesitated a moment, then stuffed the message into the pocket of her flannel shirt. If she could manage to go to Claire Holloway's, she could manage to go to the meeting. At least the licensing panel was important. She might bristle and yell when someone said the word *danger* to her, but she was no fool. Like most of the climbers who made their winter headquarters in Switzerland, she was disturbed by the rising number of accidents among novice crews climbing in the Alps. Most of those accidents were the result of inadequate guiding—and inadequate guiding, according to the members of the Committee for a Safe Mountaineering Code, was due to the fact that Switzerland had no legal provisions for licensing guides. Anybody could hang out his shingle and claim to be a guide, and almost anybody did. There was a lot of money in it.

Susan reminded herself to remind Janie to remind her that she had the meeting, and went on to the next message.

It wasn't really a message. It was a name, and, looking down at it, Susan had a powerful sense of déjà vu. Written on the tiny square of white scrap paper in Janie's rounded finishing-school scrawl was the name *Jack Cameron*.

"He called just after you left this morning," Janie said when Susan finally located her in the back of the equipment closet. "First he called, then he came and I told him where you were, then he called again. About five minutes ago, just before you came in. It was weird."

Susan picked her way over the piles of ankle weights, safety ropes, and pitons Janie had strewn across the closet floor and sat down on a packing crate.

"Weird? How?" she asked Janie. "And what did he want?"

Janie ran a hand through her short blond curls, screwed her heart-shaped face into a frown, and shook her head. "He wanted to make an appointment," she said slowly. "At least, that's what he said the first time he called this morning. I told him we were a *women's* climbing school, but it didn't seem to faze him. Then I told him it would have to be tomorrow, because you were full up today. So we made an appointment for tomorrow at three. No problem. I wrote it down in my book. Then, maybe half an hour later, he showed up at the door, wanting to know where you were. Well, you'd just left, so I told him that, but he didn't believe me. Then I told him where you'd gone, and—" Janie began to look distinctly confused. "Then the oddest thing happened," she marveled. "It was as if someone had set fire to his butt. He absolutely rocketed out of here. All I did was tell him you were making a training climb, and he acted like the Martians had landed. It was amazing."

Susan sighed, not knowing what to think or feel about any of this. It would be a lot easier, she decided, if she knew his motives. Had he followed her this morning because he was anxious to get in touch with her, or because he was convinced she would get into trouble? Should she be embarrassed or angry? And why did she have such strong emotions about the man, anyway?

"What did he want when he called back?" she asked. "To cancel the appointment?"

"No!" Janie crowed triumphantly. "That was what was so weird." She fished around in the pocket of her jeans and came up with a scrap of paper. "You tell me what this means. Quote: 'Tell Miss Reed I stand corrected if my manner was harsh, but I do not apologize. Unless I hear otherwise, I shall assume our appointment will be as scheduled.'" Janie shook her head. "Strange," she breathed.

"Very strange," Susan agreed. She stood up and stretched, wishing she didn't feel compelled to explain things to Janie. Just thinking about Jack Cameron made her feel tight and jittery. All she wanted to do was put the advanced class through attack assault training and push the memory of this morning's incident—and the disturbing possibility of another incident to come—completely out of her mind. Unfortunately, she knew she owed Janie an explanation.

Quickly she outlined the scene that morning on the mountain, skipping over the worst details of their argument and concentrating on the rescue and the way they had parted.

Oddly, Janie didn't seem the least bit intrigued by the

animosity that had sprung up between Susan and Jack. She was much more interested in the accident. "I keep telling you you have to stop climbing by yourself," she fretted. "Every time you go out there I expect to get a call saying you've broken your neck. I don't blame him for being angry with you. I'd have been angry with you, for God's sake."

"Don't swear," Susan said absently, wondering why Janie's admonitions didn't annoy her the way Jack's had. When Janie lectured her, Susan felt only warmly protected, not challenged. "I was perfectly fine," she assured the younger woman. "The piton held, the rope held, I even remembered what I was supposed to do. I just wish I'd done it instead of letting him help me back to that ledge. I'd have saved myself a lot of time, trouble, and agitation."

"You'd save *me* a lot of time, trouble, and agitation if you didn't make face ascents without a partner," Janie muttered.

"I could always train *you* to go with me," Susan teased.

Janie gave her a withering look, grabbed a box of safety belts, and got to her feet.

"You couldn't get me up on one of those mountains if you started paying double time," Janie declared. "Now get out of here and let me work. *Somebody* has to do inventory if we're not going to run out of everything it takes six weeks to get hold of."

"You have to do inventory, and I have to run a class," Susan agreed. "Maybe if we concentrate on our work, we can both forget about Jack Cameron." She walked off toward the practice room, absentmindedly shaking her joints until they felt loose and ready for exercise. She had, she thought, the perfect antidote for this morning's mental roller coaster. She would give her students a set of workouts they'd never forget, sweat herself into a case of terminal exhaustion, then jump into the shower and start dressing for Claire's party.

She wouldn't have time to think about Jack Cameron.

It didn't work. Susan led not one but two attack assault courses, paced her beginners' class on a five-mile run, and wound up the day with weight training. Not for a minute did she manage to get Jack Cameron out of her mind. She saw him strong and cool and tantalizingly sexual, the way she had first perceived him. She saw him arrogant and demanding, the way he had been on their hostile descent. Her mind replayed their argument half a dozen times. She might as well have spent the day locked in a room with him, instead of working out with a group of friendly, energetic women. He was driving her just as crazy in his absence as he had when he'd been standing two feet from her nose.

By six o'clock, when she had seen the last of her students to the door and closed it behind them, Susan was hot, sweaty, and irritable. This was ridiculous. She'd never been affected this strongly by anyone before. Even in the worst days of her marriage, she had always been able to escape from her problems with Dan by plunging herself into long periods of physical exertion. That, after all, was a good part of what exercise was for. You were supposed to concentrate on it, lose yourself in it. It was supposed to be a time apart from emotional concern.

Today the "time apart" had been nothing but an invitation to a fantasy world where arguments were re-argued until she won them and first impressions were dispelled in favor of the ones she would have liked to make. She might have been able to handle her feelings if they hadn't been so contradictory, but she couldn't make up her mind. Did she want to kill the man or impress him? And why, in the name of sanity, did it matter so much?

She slammed up the stairs to the second floor, determined to write to everyone who had ever published a book on physical fitness and tell them exactly what she thought of their platitudes about "time apart" and "losing yourself."

She found the note Janie had taped to her bedroom door, tore it down, and stalked to her closet to get her robe. DON'T FORGET CLAIRE'S, the note read. There was more scribbling at the bottom, but Susan was in no mood for details. She tossed the note onto the bed and headed for the shower.

Once there, she turned the water on as hot as it would go and stepped under the punishing stream. Then she raised her eyes to heaven and thanked Providence that she'd decided to live in Switzerland and not in Italy or France. At least the Swiss had American-style showers. If she'd had to put up with a hand-held nozzle after a day like today, she'd probably have gone up and taken a dive off the Maidenhorn.

Less than an hour later, Susan was standing in front of the full-length mirror at the far end of the second-floor hall. She was in full evening makeup, her long, thick red hair was secured at each temple and flowing gracefully over her bare shoulders, and she was beginning to wonder if her dress was about to collapse or just looked like it. The black velvet was backless and strapless, with a tightly fitted bodice and full, swirling skirt that draped to the floor. Janie called it Susan's "create-a-duel dress," implying that every man who saw her in it was catapulted into making the sort of suggestions Susan claimed she didn't want.

Whenever Janie started making those comments, Susan

patted her on the head and ignored her. She loved her black velvet gown. It was just the kind of thing that would have sent Dan into space with panic. It made her feel beautiful and mysterious and very, very daring. Besides, she'd never had trouble turning away men she didn't want. All she had to do was treat them to a few minutes of her formidable temper and most of them ran like rabbits.

Somewhere inside her a mocking little voice whispered that there was at least one man out there who might not be so easy to intimidate, but she shut it out. She had enough to worry about tonight without getting worked up about that again. The parents were waiting to be charmed, and she knew from past experience that she'd have to work overtime to do so. She could deal with whatever Jack Cameron wanted of her if he showed up at their appointment tomorrow afternoon.

The doorbell pealed, but that sound had hardly stopped before Susan heard another, more ominous noise. Breaking glass, she thought fretfully as she listened to the roof shudder under an assault of pebbles. Damn. All she needed now was a minor avalanche. She'd be held up for hours.

Momentarily ignoring the doorbell, she hurried down the hall, checked the bedroom windows, then started for the stairs. Avalanches in this part of the Alps were almost never serious, but they created myriad small problems for the tiny wooden chalets that lined the slopes. Somewhere in her house a window was broken, letting cold air into a high-ceilinged building that was difficult to keep warm under the best of circumstances. She'd have to find the break and repair it before she left. If she didn't, she'd come home to an inhospitably cold house, some snow-damaged furniture, and a heating bill large enough to break her budget for the season.

The doorbell rang again as Susan began to descend

to the first floor. She quickened her step, her nerves raw with frustration. Who could possibly be ringing her bell at this hour? Granted, many of her rich students were spoiled and inconsiderate, and they had a tendency to leave their belongings in the locker rooms and then show up at odd hours to retrieve them. Even so, they usually disturbed her in the mornings. Evenings in Bresson during the climbing season were too full of opportunities for partying to waste.

She paused on the next to the last step and momentarily considered ignoring the doorbell and pretending she wasn't home. But if it were one of her students at the door, she'd have help looking for that broken window. If it were one of her nicer students, she might even have help fixing it.

She hurried the rest of the way to the door, tugging at her bodice with one hand and trying to tame a few straying strands of hair with the other. At the last minute she stopped, carefully ran her fingers over the combs in her hair, and tightened them over some tendrils that were loose.

Which was how it came to pass that she was a picture of perfection when she opened the door to Jack Cameron.

It was a good thing, too. *He* looked like an ad for the ultimate in men's formal wear.

He even had a very large, very black Mercedes waiting in the drive.

Chapter 3

MAYBE IT WAS because she had been thinking of him all day, or maybe it was because the last few minutes had been so fraught, but Susan wasn't really surprised to see him in her doorway. Jack, on the other hand, seemed stunned. His eyes traveled slowly over her wavy tresses and bare shoulders, then fastened on her tightly outlined bosom. His jaw was slack, his eyes wide and darkly intense. Susan began to get the feeling he could see through the soft fabric of her dress. She felt the heat of a blush rising slowly into her face as a strange, insistent tingling began just beneath her skin. She would not have been entirely shocked to look down and find herself naked. She *felt* naked under Jack's rapt scrutiny—naked and vulnerable in ways that went far beyond the physical.

He raised his eyes and caught her glance.

"Beautiful," he murmured, reaching out to brush his fingers against her collarbone.

His touch was like a sudden spurt of white-hot flame. Instinctively, Susan drew back. There was something wrong with this scene, her mind warned her. But the alarm sounded dully through senses already overloaded with more dangerous, more provocative sensations. *Moth to flame,* came the mocking echo of reason as it fought vainly with her involuntary, undeniable response to Jack's small exploratory caress. *Moth to flame . . .*

Breaking glass.

It was a very faint sound, but it changed everything. Susan whirled, as much in an attempt to hide her face from Jack as to determine the source of the noise. How could she lose control of herself so easily? she thought furiously. Especially with this man! Undeniably he was attractive. She'd found him so from the moment she saw him. But she was mature enough to know that mere physical attraction could not make up for lack of mutual respect. Jack Cameron had spent nearly an hour this morning making it perfectly clear how little he respected her in the area she cared about most—her climbing. It was *that* she should be thinking of, not the way his eyes gleamed in the darkness or the way his rough fingertips burned against the base of her throat. She was a grown woman. She had loved and lost. She knew about these things.

You've never known anything like that, the small voice inside her cautioned. Susan violently pushed the thought away.

"There's a rock shower." Her voice came out in a tight little chirp as she kept her back turned toward Jack. "A window's broken somewhere."

She knew her words didn't begin to explain the situation, but she hurried away anyway, determined to put as much space between the man and herself as the chalet afforded. She needed a chance to organize her thoughts. Once she was on an even keel again, she could ask him what he was doing here and find a way to get rid of him. She *did* want to get rid of him, she was sure.

She checked the windows in the kitchen and was on her way to the deck room she had converted to a dance studio when he caught up with her.

"Just a minute," he snapped, grabbing her arm.

She pulled away from him, backing into the wall and folding her arms across her chest in a gesture of protection. The way the man looked at her was indecent. It turned her muscles to water. She didn't need any of that weakness now.

"There's a window broken," she repeated, forcing her voice into something that barely resembled coldly polite self-control. "I've got to find out where it is and fix it."

Jack's eyebrows quirked sardonically. "In that dress?" he taunted. "In high heels?"

Susan nearly stamped her foot. "I could fix a broken window on stilts," she sputtered, wondering if he'd come up here just to give her another list of all the things he didn't think she could do. "Now if you'll just get out of my way—"

Jack held up his hands in surrender and stepped aside. "Go right ahead," he told her. "I didn't come up here to fight, I promise."

Susan gave him a disbelieving look. "What did you come up here for?" she demanded. "It's Friday night, you know. I'm not exactly open for business."

Jack impatiently ran a hand through his thick blond hair. "I left a message," he told her. "With that assistant of yours. We've got business to discuss. I didn't want to wait until tomorrow."

"So you show up in—in that?" Susan gestured to his tuxedo. "You don't exactly look ready for a discussion of the relative merits of free-breath versus tank-control ascents."

Jack shrugged. "As I said, I left a message. Miss Dean said you were going out to Claire Holloway's. I was going out to Claire Holloway's. The perfect solution seemed to be for me to pick you up and take you there. How was I supposed to know she'd forget to leave a message?"

"Janie never forgets—" Susan began. Then she bit her lip. There had been all that extra writing she hadn't bothered to read at the bottom of the note Janie had left on her bedroom door. If she walked upstairs right now, she'd undoubtedly find a nice little explanation of when Jack was arriving and why.

Damn. The last thing she wanted was to spend more time in a pointless battle of wills. There was work to do. There seemed to be a cold draft coming in from the dance studio, and if the problem was in there, Susan knew it was going to take half the night to fix it.

"Now that you're here, you might as well help," she said brusquely, trying to conceal her nervousness. Affecting casual nonchalance, she brushed by Jack, hurried to the end of the hall, grabbed the antique metal door handle, and pulled at it in agitation, alarmed at the waves of frigid air swirling under her dress.

"It's freezing in here," she muttered distractedly to Jack.

"Hmm," he agreed. "What broke? A wall?"

Susan reached out and found the light switch.

"Skylights," she sighed as the room was bathed in the harsh glare of arc lights. "Half a ceiling full of skylights."

"You can't climb a ladder in those shoes," Jack was still insisting half an hour later. "I won't let you climb a ladder in those shoes."

Susan stopped below the first of the broken skylight panes and carefully set the heavy, age-grayed wooden stepladder on the floor. Then she closed her eyes and counted very slowly to ten. That seemed to be her basic reaction to Jack Cameron. No matter what else he made her feel, she always ended up counting.

She pulled the ladder open and balanced it upright, trying to think of the best way to say what she had to say. She was cold, her dress was covered with dust, and her hair was doing the funky frizz. She was not, however, angry. It was odd the way only half an hour of uninterrupted exposure to a man could temper one's reactions to him, she thought. She no longer wanted to kill Jack Cameron; she simply wanted to get rid of him.

"Look," she said, leaning against the ladder's splintered flank. "In the past half hour you have expressed the following: first, that I was never going to get down the cellar stairs in these heels; second, that I was never going to get back up the cellar stairs in these heels, especially carrying this ladder; third, that if I tried to carry this ladder down the hall to the studio in these heels, I'd break my neck. Here I am, neck unbroken. Why don't you just give up?"

Jack frowned, looking like a much-put-upon little boy whose every attempt to do the right thing had resulted in disaster. The expression was surprisingly appealing, and Susan turned away, distressed to find herself warming to the man. He looked so vulnerable, so innocent, she had an almost irrepressible urge to comfort him. Hastily she began to ascend the ladder. She not only had altitude sickness, she decided; the disease was apparently terminal.

"Why don't you hold the ladder for me?" she suggested as the wooden contraption wobbled unsteadily beneath her. "You can hand me the panes as I need them."

Jack's hand instantly went to the side of the ladder. Feeling its frame shudder, Susan sucked in her breath, then let it out again as the ladder came to a solid, anchored rest. She wouldn't be caught dead admitting it, but Jack might have a point about this one. Her high, thin spikes made it difficult to balance on the warped rungs, and the incessant wobbling of the frame would have made her seasick if Jack's hold hadn't stopped it. It did nothing for her equilibrium to realize she would never have been up on this ladder in these shoes if Jack hadn't goaded her into it. Under ordinary circumstances, she would have changed into jeans and sneakers before even attempting a repair job on the skylights.

She leaned down and took one of the panes he was holding up for her.

"Skylights are very important for dance practice," she told him brightly, determined to ignore the queasy flutter that had started in her stomach. Like many climbers, she wasn't particularly fond of heights. It was the knowledge that she was protected by ropes and pitons that made her feel safe on a mountain. "Dance practice is essential for women climbers," she continued. "It lengthens the muscles and strengthens the legs. We use it instead of the fourth series of workouts in the Bernheimer method program."

"You're tampering with the Bernheimer?" Jack sounded horrified. "But it took over a hundred years to develop that program! It was devised from the recommendations of the best climbers in history!"

Susan sighed, leaning over to get another pane. At least the replacements were going to be easy to make. The first pane had slid into its mooring with the ease of butter gliding over hot toast. With the number of minor rock slides this part of the Alps was subjected to every year, she'd certainly made the right decision when she put out the money for this new system. Replacing the old skylights had required a complicated process of fitting and puttying.

As for this new tack of Jack's, it wasn't anything she hadn't heard before. Even the Swiss government had had objections when she first explained her plans for the new Women's Alpine Climbing School's training program.

Feeling on sure ground for the first time since she'd met Jack that morning, Susan allowed a sliver of annoyance to inch to the surface of her consciousness.

"The Bernheimer method," she explained, her tone as patient and condescending as the one he'd used to lecture her on the mountain, "was devised *by* men *for* men. There's a series meant to lower the body's center of gravity, which women don't need, because they already have a lower center of gravity. There isn't any exercise at all to lengthen the muscles, because men's muscles are already long enough. All the Bernheimer method does for women is exaggerate an already exaggerated tendency to develop a fat ass."

There was silence—one of Jack's patented silences that went on too long. Susan looked down at the thoughtful, worried expression on his face and frowned. She had expected him to be scornful or angry, or even shocked at the earthiness of her expression—anything but thoughtful. That she hadn't been remotely capable of predicting his response made her even queasier than her dubious perch did. She leaned over and grabbed the last of the panes, hoping to hide the perverse flare of resentment she couldn't quite control. She knew it wasn't rational to feel that Jack was purposely foiling her attempt to understand him, but nothing she felt around Jack Cameron was rational. He acted, and she went off like a firecracker left out in the hot July sun.

She slipped the last pane into place, gathered her skirt around her knees, and hurried gratefully to the floor. At least one thing had gone right, she thought. She hadn't fallen and made a fool out of herself, or lost her courage and allowed him to fix the skylights for her. He need never know how close she'd come to admitting the wisdom of his sarcastic advice.

"I've got to clean up now," she told him as she folded up the ladder and tucked it awkwardly under her arm. "I'm due at a party—"

Jack waved his hand impatiently. "So am I," he reminded her. "But we're never going to get there. Everyone clears out of those things by ten, and it's nine o'clock already. We might as well skip it and get down to business."

Susan stared at the face of the elegant gold evening watch he offered for her edification. "Damn," she said. "Janie's going to kill me. I promised her I'd make it tonight."

"It doesn't matter," Jack said dismissively. "There's a party at Claire's almost every week. You can go to the next one."

"It matters to me," Susan said firmly, brushing by him with the ladder hooked over her hip. "The Women's Alpine Climbing School is a business as well as a school, Mr. Cameron. I can't afford to make enemies of the tourists."

"You can't afford to make enemies of the serious climbers, either," Jack said, allowing his face to break into a reluctant grin. He looked good that way, too, Susan thought helplessly. She was beginning to think there were no circumstances under which he wouldn't look good. He reached out and swung the ladder out of her arms before she had a chance to protest. "Go up and get washed off," he ordered. "I'll put this back in the basement for you. Then we can talk."

"Talk about what?" Susan demanded automatically, although she knew her voice lacked its earlier imperiousness. She didn't know if she was tired of fighting him or just plain tired, but she did know she was too close to exhaustion to want to stage another scene. Even so, she didn't want Jack Cameron to think he could push her around. She was convinced that once he started, he'd be a hard man to stop. She'd already had adequate evidence of just how hard in his behavior on the mountain.

"Talk about what?" she repeated in the face of his silence. "I don't think we're going to agree on anything, Mr. Cameron," she offered warily.

"Wrong!" Jack's smile was full, open, triumphant. "Here's one thing we agree on," he said. "The Bernheimer method. I think you're right. It probably isn't a good way to train women for mountain climbing. Bernheimer himself said the method was devised to make men's bodies more like women's, because the perfect physical specimen for mountain climbing was a women who was twenty pounds too heavy for fashion but in Olympic-training shape."

"What?" Susan demanded, stopping dead in her tracks. Jack Cameron acquiescing to something she'd said? She could hardly have been more shocked if he'd ripped off his clothes and started doing an Irish jig on the glass-strewn dance studio floor.

Glass. She had to do something about the glass. She headed for the broom closet. She felt giddy and more than a little piqued. "You spend every waking second in my company telling me what I'm doing wrong," she muttered. "Then you come out with—with *this*, for heaven's sake."

"What's wrong with it?" Jack asked innocently. "You're not exactly twenty pounds too heavy for fashion"—he gave her an appreciative smile—"but then, Bernheimer was living in the anorexic 1920s. Besides, I like you the way you are. And I don't mind admitting when someone's right. It's only common decency."

"Only common decency," Susan repeated. The man wasn't only exasperating, she decided; he was a lunatic.

"Go put that thing in the basement," she told him as she forced herself *not* to count ten. "I'll sweep and wash up, and then we can talk."

"I'll make it worth your while," he promised as he turned and marched toward the door.

Susan watched him go with mixed feelings. The man made no sense, she told herself.

Twenty minutes later Susan was sitting on the ragged, spring-pocked couch in the living room, feeling like the protagonist of one of the odder episodes of *The Twilight Zone*. Jack had taken off his jacket, tie, and vest and was lying on the worn red carpet, making neat piles out of the stack of papers he'd taken from his briefcase. The briefcase had materialized, apparently, out of thin air, while Susan was upstairs changing.

"The east face of the Maidenhorn," Jack was saying. "It's never been done. Nobody's even come close. That's the beauty of this. I spent the last six weeks wandering around that mountain, trying to figure out a way. And I've found it." He gave her a smile that was both rueful and proud. "It's a killer course," he said, "but it's do-able. It'll take the best trained, best equipped, best mentally prepared crew in the world, but it's do-able."

Susan nodded and sipped her coffee. The Maidenhorn was the only mountain in the Alps directly accessible from the village of Bresson, and it was such a difficult climb that few mountaineers attempted even its south, or "easy," face.

What Jack wanted to discuss had been obvious from the moment she reentered her living room, dressed in jeans and a flannel shirt and absurdly pleased that he had made coffee. She knew an expedition report when she saw one. The mere sight of those papers spread across her floor gave her a thrill. Since buying the chalet and starting the school, Susan had had very few chances to sit in on the planning of a major expedition. She had also had few chances to display the depth of her mountaineering expertise.

Sitting cross-legged with her mug balanced on her ankles, she drew all the authority of her ten years as a climber and three as a teacher around her like a cloak. Since Jack probably wanted to consult her on the training of the women in his crew, she knew she should be reveling in this chance to advance her own reputation and that of her school. She should feel flattered. Instead, she was simply relieved to find what she knew would be an effective buffer between them. Armed with cool professionalism, she was sure she could minimize the unsettling effect he had on her. She would, she told herself, finally be in control.

"You're going to need a backer," she cautioned Jack. "That'll be an expensive climb. And backers are hard to find at this time of year. Most of the advertising companies decided last spring which climbs they wanted to back."

"I know that." Jack brushed a swatch of hair from his eyes. "I don't need a backer this time. I've written a couple of mountaineering handbooks and a Himalaya guide. They're doing fairly well. I can back this climb myself. Besides"—he shrugged—"I did talk to the advertising boys. I'm afraid..." He raised his hands in a gesture of futility.

"I know." Susan grimaced sympathetically. "They don't want any part of something that might fail. Or where somebody might get hurt. It's bad for business."

"No one's ever been hurt on one of my crews," Jack said stubbornly. "I've seen to that."

Susan felt her mouth tugging down into a most unsympathetic scowl, so she sipped her coffee again and contorted her features back into something resembling bland interest. She finally had Jack where she wanted him—in a civilized conversation that engaged her emotions not at all—and she wanted to keep it that way.

"If you've got the money, all you have to do is go up," she said, trying to sound enthusiastic. "If you make it, it'll be quite a coup. You'll be more famous than you already are."

"So will you," Jack said coaxingly. He leaped to his feet, apparently too restless to stay still a moment longer. "I've been trying to figure out how to talk you into this for a whole week. I hadn't seen you then, but that didn't matter. I looked into your record after Mary Agnes Morabito told me about you," he said, naming one of the few women Alpine master climbers. "I know you've made only all-women crew ascents in the Alps, and if that's some kind of political decision that's important to you, that's your business. But think how good a climb like this will be for your school. It could make the whole operation an instant, resounding success."

Susan blinked. The funny feeling was coming back again, the odd seasickness that meant Jack had managed to trick her into one of his roller-coaster rides again.

"Climb?" she asked him incredulously, wanting to kick herself for thinking she had managed to get the situation under control. She would never get this man safely labeled and filed away. He wouldn't stay in one place long enough. "How can you ask me to climb?" she demanded. "What about this morning? You could have been wearing a sign painted in Day-Glo, it was so obvious you thought I was an amateur!"

He stopped pacing, shoved his hands into his pockets, and frowned down at her. "I never said you were an amateur. This morning—well, that was this morning. It was a stupid thing to do—"

"Don't tell me I'm stupid," Susan snapped.

"I'm not!" Jack snapped back. "For Pete's sake, Susan. I looked at two hundred dossiers, trying to select the right crew for this climb. I'm not picking amateurs— this whole thing is much too important for me, and I've got a record I don't want to destroy. Believe me, I liked the way you looked on paper. You've got one of the most impressive ascent records of any woman in the Alps. You've got excellent recommendations from the crews you've climbed with. I knew two months ago I wanted you on this team."

"I suppose you think the reality doesn't quite live up to the paper record," Susan said stiffly, trying not to sound mollified.

"Not true," Jack insisted. "I watched your descent this morning. You're a wonderful natural climber, one of the best I've ever seen. You have a feeling for the mountains, and that's the most important thing. You're well trained, too. Even if you do take unacceptable chances—"

"There was nothing unacceptable, as you put it, about that *chance*," Susan began hotly. "I was just—"

Jack waved it away. "We've been through all that," he said dismissively. "The fact is, I've been investigating possibilities for this crew for months, and I want you to make this climb with us. You're one of the best, and I need the best. And you're a woman, and I need women, too." When Susan looked surprised, he laughed ruefully. "I'm in business, too," he explained. "I write books on mountaineering. If they sell, I live well. If not, I don't. So far I've been lucky."

"I think *Field Guide to Himalaya* was more than lucky," Susan said wryly. "That thing must have made you a mint."

"I'm not starving," Jack admitted. "But let's face it. The better my name is known, the better my books sell. Women in mountain climbing make great press these days. Exciting reading, tie-ins with the women's movement—it's all there." He reached out to touch the curling red tendrils of her hair. "You'd make a great photograph, too," he told her. "Better than the *Sports Illustrated* swimsuit parade."

Susan shifted uneasily. She knew she should feel more than flattered by this kind of talk, but a part of her didn't want to hear it. Besides, she didn't like him standing over her that way. He made her feel much too small, much too open, when he towered over her. She had a fleeting memory of the way things had been when she first opened the door to him that evening, and she instinctively hugged her knees to her chest.

"I don't think I could climb a mountain with you telling me to be careful every spare minute," she said slowly, avoiding his eyes and working overtime to keep her voice steady. "I nearly brained you back there in the studio, and that wasn't even anything important."

Jack clucked. "I wouldn't spend all my time telling you to be careful," he said reasonably. "I was worried about you on that ladder. I was worried about you on that mountain this morning, too. Nobody in his right mind makes a face ascent alone."

"Except you," Susan said resentfully.

"I thought I'd explained that," he said in obvious exasperation.

"You did," Susan agreed. "But that's not the point. It wasn't just the way you lectured me. It was also the descent and the way you've been behaving since you got here tonight. You simply don't trust me or my abilities."

"Is that what you thought was going on on that mountain?" Jack demanded, the red of anger flaring into his cheeks. "You thought I was playing some kind of stupid macho game?"

"I don't know what you were doing," Susan said defensively, a little awed by his sudden intensity. "And it really doesn't matter. All I'm trying to tell you is that I don't think we can work together—on a climb or anything else."

"No?" It was a single, softly spoken word, but it carried a depth and breadth of meaning Susan couldn't begin to decipher. Seeing Jack start toward her, she scurried off the couch and began backing toward the door.

"I think you'd better leave," she said in a strangled voice. "I think—"

"Let me tell you what *I* think," Jack said purposefully. His hand shot out and circled her wrist, pulling her insistently toward him. Suddenly Susan found herself pressed to him, her cheek rubbing against the starched, scratchy whiteness of his dress shirt. He leaned down toward her, cupping her face in his hands, his fingers splaying through the disarrayed locks of her hair.

"What I think," he began, anger and wry amusement warring for supremacy in his eyes, "is that I just went out to get my briefcase. And when I did, I checked the car. It was quite a rock slide, Susan Reed. It felled a tree."

"What do you mean?" she asked him tremulously, thinking that she ought to break his hold and run, but unable to make herself move.

His smile was sardonic, challenging, but his voice was a husky whisper. "I mean, there's a tree across your driveway. I can't get out. I think I'm just going to have to spend the night."

She opened her mouth to protest just as his head

swooped down to hers. Much to her surprise, instead of issuing a passionate refusal, she found herself accepting the salty probing of his tongue.

It was like drowning, or falling from a very high place. Susan felt the strong hands on her back, the hard, tense muscles of Jack's thighs against her own. A fire started deep within her and began spreading outward, engulfing every millimeter of skin and nerve. She pressed herself against the broad expanse of his chest, wanting to melt into the enveloping warmth of the man.

"We've got the whole night," Jack whispered as his tongue teased the sensitive hollows of her ear.

"You can't stay here all night," Susan protested weakly, shuddering as his lips began to trail slowly along the base of her neck. "You have to go home," she said, feeling dazed.

"I don't have to go home," Jack urged softly. "I can stay here with you. Can't you tell how good we'd be together?"

His hands began to explore her back under the thin flannel shirt, and Susan felt herself twisting toward him, giving him more and more access. Her conscious mind was faintly sputtering: *You can't, you can't, you can't.* Her body was like a runaway train. Her responses flared and raged, irrational, undeniable, uncontrollable. She wanted to touch every inch of him, to have him touch every inch of her. She wanted to silence her conscious mind and listen only to what her body was demanding of her.

Jack's arms circled her, crushing her against him. "Dear heaven," he moaned. "I knew it would be like this. I knew it the minute I saw you."

The words fell on her ears like an ice cube into a cup of boiling water. The effects were minimal at first, but gradually escalated. Susan's shift of mood was palpable;

her body seemed to go from hot to cold, from violent to still. A small part of her wanted to recapture the abandon of a few moments before, but it was impossible. *The moment I saw you,* she thought, and she was unable to banish a mental snapshot of their meeting on the mountain.

Suddenly she felt raw and angry, betrayed. What had she been thinking of? How could she submit so readily to a man she hardly knew, a man who had spent most of their short time together insulting her? That he had ended up flattering her didn't matter. She knew the seeds of contempt were there.

"What's the matter?" Jack demanded.

Susan looked up into the dark sternness of his eyes. His body had become as rigid as her own, and the arms that encircled her shoulders were no longer warmly enveloping; they were viselike.

Panicked, Susan pulled away, surprised and a little disappointed at the ease with which Jack let her go. She felt a spurt of what she knew was unreasonable anger. How could he release her so quickly when just a moment ago he had been so passionate, so demanding? Could he turn his passion on and off as if it were a faucet?

She stood away from him, compulsively smoothing her hair and her clothes. "I'll get you a sleeping bag," she said, her shaky voice attesting to her still turbulent confusion. She turned away and started for the hall. "You can bed down in the weight room. That's what I use when I play hostel to visiting climbers."

"That's what I'm supposed to consider myself?" Jack asked harshly. "A visiting climber in need of a hostel?"

Susan couldn't stop herself from turning around. She paused at the door to the hall, leaning against the frame for support and forcibly resisting his commanding allure. "That's all you are," she said in as even a tone as she could manage. "And that's all you're going to be."

He was big and he was fast. He reached her before the second sentence was fully past her lips. He gripped her wrist and held it. "You shouldn't lie to yourself," he told her firmly. "It's a dangerous pastime."

There was a long moment of silence between them before Susan abruptly broke his hold. This was no time for good manners, she decided. When he came this close, her body was too open to him, too ready to betray her.

"The sleeping bags are in the equipment room," she bit out, hating herself for sounding so breathless.

Then she turned and fled.

Chapter 4

THE PHONE RANG at six-thirty the next morning, Saturday. Susan made a purely instinctive leap out of bed, knocking the clock, the lamp, the phone, and an open package of Band-aids off the night table, and landed in a heap on the floor. Everything else landed there with her. Band-aids were scattered like confetti. Tiny shards of the light bulb glistened on the floor. The clock had stopped.

She knew it was Saturday because there was no sock over the left rear poster of her four-poster bed. She always put a sock over the poster on the mornings she had to get up—to remind her she had to get up. She knew it was six-thirty because that was the last thing the clock had registered.

The phone had stopped ringing and began emitting squawks from the receiver. She reached for it and discovered an empty champagne bottle lying on its side. She picked it up and stared at it. Ridiculous, she thought. She didn't drink. She hadn't had more than five glasses of wine in her entire life.

Then why did her head hurt so badly? she wondered. And why did her eyes feel like inflated balloons?

Something that sounded like a wail came from the receiver. Exasperated, Susan snatched it up. "Women's Alpine Climbing School," she announced grouchily, forgetting that the phone in her bedroom rang only on her private number, not on the business number of the school. "We're closed."

"Susan?" Janie Dean asked tentatively.

"For Pete's sake!" Susan exploded. She regretted it immediately. Her head couldn't have hurt more if she'd been run over by a truck. "Do you realize what time it is?" she asked Janie in a softer tone. "It's Saturday."

"I know it's Saturday," Janie said patiently. "But Mr. Cameron called about his suitcase, and it sounded so odd, and besides, how was I supposed to know you weren't awake? I mean, under the circumstances..."

"Under what circumstances?" Susan asked desperately. As far as she was concerned, Janie wasn't making any sense. One of the things she'd said, however, sent off warning bells. *Mr. Cameron.* There was something very ominous about that innocent sounding "Mr. Cameron." If only she could remember what.

She took a deep breath and tackled the conversation again. "Start from the beginning," she instructed Janie. "Go very slowly."

"Mr. Cameron called about his suitcase," Janie ventured.

"That isn't the beginning," Susan said impatiently.

"But it is," Janie assured her. "Not more than five minutes ago. I was already up. I mean, I intended to get to the chalet by seven-thirty and work on some of that inventory I started yesterday, so I was getting dressed. And the phone rang, and it was our concierge, and then it was Mr. Cameron. Do you follow me so far?"

"Yes," Susan said slowly. "Yes, I follow you."

"Good. Well, Mr. Cameron wanted his suitcase. He said all he had with him were his evening clothes. So I went to his room—he's staying in the hotel I'm in—and got it. I had to have the concierge help, you understand, but he'd called her, too, so she was ready for me. Susan, it's a really big suitcase."

There was a pause. Susan rubbed her fingers over her lips. They felt dry and chapped. Her neck ached. Her back ached. Her head was ready to split apart. But she was beginning to remember.

"You know," Janie said in a wounded little voice, "this makes more sense to me than it seems to make to you. This suitcase thing is huge. It has to hold enough for a couple of months. I'm going to have to hire a taxi just to get it up there."

"Don't do that," Susan said quickly. "Put the suitcase back in Mr. Cameron's room and leave it there."

"I can't put it back in Mr. Cameron's room," Janie protested. "I'd have to get the concierge again, and she's unhappy with me already. Besides, the hotel is serving breakfast now, and—"

"Then leave it in your room," Susan told her. "I don't care if you throw it out your window. Just don't bring it up here."

"I won't," Janie promised. "But, Susan, are you sure you're all right? I mean, you sound sort of fuzzy."

"I'm drunk," Susan said carelessly.

"At six o'clock in the morning?" Janie sounded shocked.

"Not drunk," Susan corrected. "Afterdrunk. Sick from drinking. Something."

"Hung over," Janie said with some amusement.

"Right," Susan affirmed.

"I'll see you in an hour," Janie said cheerfully. "Swallow an egg."

The line went dead before Susan could ask Janie what she meant, but it was just as well. The very idea of an egg—any kind of egg—was enough to make her ill. And she couldn't afford to be ill now. Jack was somewhere in the chalet, making phone calls, making breakfast, making trouble, she was sure. He'd made enough trouble just by calling the Hotel Bresson and getting in touch with Janie. Before breakfast was over everyone in the village would know where he'd spent the night.

- There had been a rock slide, Susan remembered painfully. A tree had come down across her drive and blocked his car, making it impossible for him to leave. She had given him floor space in the weight room and told him where the sleeping bags were stored. If anybody asked, she would tell them that that was what had happened. It was the truth.

It was the truth, but it wasn't the half of it. Carefully, Susan replaced the receiver in the cradle. She could remember his kiss, the sweet-and-salty exploration of his tongue, the velvet-and-steel caress of his long, strong fingers. For a moment he had made her feel ready and eager for anything that might happen between them. She had been lost in the heat and honey of it. Her body had strained toward his. Her hands had roved across his back, wanting to touch him everywhere, to discover the fullness of his strength and softness. He kissed the planes and hollows of her neck, making her tingle with delight and anticipation. She could have lived forever in that kiss— if she could have stopped herself from thinking.

"Mind over matter," Susan mumbled to herself now. She got slowly to her feet, started for the door, then turned and headed for the closet. She was wearing her favorite teddy-bear pajamas, hardly the costume for declaring war. She grabbed her yellow terry-cloth robe from its hook just inside the closet door and wrapped it around herself. She had *not* lived forever in his kiss. She had come to her senses. She had told him off and given him a place to sleep and stormed to her room and locked herself in—with a bottle of champagne.

The champagne had been in the refrigerator, a half-forgotten gift from the parents of a student. Susan remembered thinking that a glass or two would help her get to sleep. Since she wouldn't have needed help getting to sleep if it hadn't been for Jack's outrageous behavior, she could blame her hangover on him, as well as—as whatever it was he was up to now.

She tightened the belt around her waist. She was going to find out exactly what he thought he was pulling, asking Janie for his suitcase. As if she'd allow him to move in!

Then, headache or no headache, she was going to kill him.

"Headache or no headache" was easier said than done, Susan discovered. The pain was excruciating, and the longer it went on the more nauseated she felt. She checked the weight room, where Jack had left his borrowed sleeping bag carefully rolled up on a bench. Then she checked the equipment room. Then she checked the kitchen. There was no sign of him anywhere.

She was on her way to the second-floor bathroom when she heard the whistling. She stopped to listen, trying to decide whether to head straight for the sound or make a pit stop for aspirin. Then she recognized the tune, and her anger began to boil over once again. "Whistle While You Work." Anyone who could make such a loud and vigorous racket whistling "Whistle While You Work" on a morning like this had to be a maniac or a fiend.

She launched herself toward the noise. The man never quit, she thought furiously. She'd just managed to absorb the shock of one of his stunts when he pulled another. She had to stop this nonsense now, forever. If she didn't, heaven only knew what he'd think of next.

She turned in at the door of the office, fully intending to pick up the nearest piece of furniture and end Jack's whistling once and for all. For one thing, the whistling was making her headache worse. For another—

She was halfway across the office before it began to sink in. Then she stopped, stood very still, and began to look cautiously around her. It was impossible. He couldn't have done this. He had no right to do this. He must have worked all night.

The vaguely insane jumble that had formerly characterized the office was gone. Papers were neatly arranged in files or resting in folders on the tops of filing cabinets and bookcases. Her desk was clean, every pen and pencil placed with orderly precision in one of three cardboard cylinders—blue pens, black pens, and pencils, Susan realized.

She peered curiously into the half-troubled, half-angry face Jack presented to her. He didn't look tired, she thought irrelevantly. She knew she should be angry, but at the moment she was too stunned to summon up the energy. The whole situation was overwhelming.

It was clearly not overwhelming to Jack, however. His expression hardened, and he stood up. "I'm glad you're here," he said evenly, looking ready to explode. "I've been at this for over an hour—"

"At what?" Susan interrupted, annoyance finally

breaking through her confusion and hangover fog. "What are you doing in my office?"

"What have *you* been doing in your office?" Jack riposted. "I walked in here this morning looking for a pencil, and I found, I found—" He threw his hands up in defeat. "There were Girl Scout cookies in one of your file drawers," he said in disgust. "I don't even want to guess how old they were."

"If I want to keep Girl Scout cookies in my drawer," Susan said angrily, "I'll keep them there. It's my office. What you're doing in it, I don't know, but—"

"What I'm doing in it is saving your life," Jack said furiously. "Just look at *these.*" He grabbed a sheaf of papers from the desk and waved them under her nose, the jerky motion making her feel dizzy and nauseated all over again. "Tax returns," he muttered ominously. "Unfiled tax returns."

"It's not illegal not to file tax returns in Switzerland," Susan told him coldly. "Not that I make enough to pay taxes in this country anyway. And not that it's any of your business!"

"Who's talking about Switzerland?" Jack demanded. He waved the papers again, and again Susan felt an uneasy ripple through her body. Then he turned away and threw the forms onto the desk. "I'm talking about your United States tax returns. If you're a U.S. citizen, you have to file—every year, no matter where you live, no matter how much money you make. Unless you make less than four hundred dollars, and I won't believe that."

"I don't care what you believe," Susan flared. "My income is none of your damn business. And neither is the way I run this office. What makes you think you've got the right to come in here and disturb all my papers, set up some system you think I ought to be following, and then start screaming at me because I don't thank you for the intrusion?"

"To hell with the intrusion," Jack erupted. "I'm talking about going to jail. If you don't file these papers, you're going to go to jail. Even if—"

"That's it," Susan said coldly. She closed her eyes to stop the room from spinning, then opened them again. Jack was still standing tensely before her, his arms rigid at his sides, his jaw locked in stubbornness.

There seemed to be a glint of something else in his eyes, something almost like amusement, but she ignored it. She was furious, more furious than she had ever been at anyone in her life. The man had no right to walk in and take over like this, no right to lecture her, no right to assume that simply because she didn't do things the way he would, she had to be incompetent, stupid, or worse.

"This is *my* business," she told Jack, her voice as even as she could make it with her stomach churning and her head floating. "This is *my* life," she went on. "I don't care how you think I ought to do things. I don't care what you think I ought to be careful of. I don't care what you consider proper professional or personal deportment. I don't want to hear another word about what you think I'm capable of doing—on the slopes or in my office. I'm all grown up, Mr. Cameron. I know my talents and my limitations, and I know how to live with both. I'm doing quite well, thank you. I don't need your help, and I don't need your criticisms." She snatched the papers from the desk and dropped them deliberately to the floor.

"I liked my mess the way it was," she continued icily. "And as for you . . ." She put a hand to her head. It was getting worse, she decided. She'd better get an aspirin soon. She looked up to see Jack eyeing her curiously.

"I'm feeling a little ill," she said stiffly, "so if you'd just get yourself together and get out of here—"

"Before I cure your hangover?" Jack teased.

Susan glared up at him suspiciously. The man could change moods faster than a chameleon could change colors, she thought disgustedly. Now he was positively grinning at her.

"If you think you can charm me out of the mood I'm in," she warned him, "you're wrong." She remembered another grievance. "And as for that stunt you pulled this morning—"

"It wasn't a stunt," Jack interrupted. Then he took her arm. "Word of honor," he said, "I *can* cure you of that hangover. You can repay the favor by listening to me."

"I'll repay the favor by not killing you," Susan grumbled. "That ought to be enough."

Susan squinted at the glass in front of her, picked it up, held it up to the light, squinted again, and put it down. She wasn't going to drink that thing, she decided. It looked revolting. Besides, she was angry. At least underneath the nausea she was angry. Unfortunately, the nausea seemed to cancel out everything else. She couldn't concentrate on being angry.

She pushed the glass away from her. "I can't drink this," she complained. "It has an egg in it."

Jack dropped into the chair beside her and smiled. "Of course it's got an egg in it," he said cheerfully. "Also Worcestershire sauce. Also—"

"Never mind," Susan said quickly, feeling her stomach heave. "I don't want the recipe." She looked resentfully around the kitchen. It had been Jack's idea to come down here, and she was sure it was a mistake. Everything in the room was bright yellow and white, a choice she'd once thought would make the room look larger and cheerier. Now it merely looked glaring. It hurt her eyes.

"Why don't you just say what you have to say?" she asked Jack, fumbling for the anger that had served her so well earlier. She told herself it would come back eventually, and probably redoubled. After all, his invasion of her office had been inexcusable.

Jack pushed the glass close to her again. "Drink it," he ordered. "Then please consider accepting my apologies for this morning. You were right about one thing: I didn't have the right to reorganize your office. That was out of bounds."

"Can't you be consistent?" Susan exploded. She immediately regretted her vehemence. Her head ready to burst, she grabbed the glass and gulped down the concoction, hoping it wouldn't taste too terrible. Fortunately, it didn't taste of anything at all. She put it down on the table and turned to Jack again. "I would very much appreciate it," she said more calmly, "if you could just try to behave in a consistent manner. What am I supposed to think of the things you do?"

Jack grinned. "Look at it this way," he suggested. "I've got a mania for order. Sometimes it gets out of hand."

"If you've got such a mania for order, you ought to stay out of rooms with closed doors," Susan offered.

"That door was wide open," Jack said ruefully. There was a whistling from the stove, and he got up to take the kettle off the heat. "How's your head?"

"Still wretched." Then she admitted grudgingly, "My stomach's a little calmer."

"Good." Jack returned to the table with coffee and toast and set it down before her. "Now," he said, sitting down again, "since we have the apology out of the way, can we get down to business?"

Susan dumped three teaspoons of sugar into her coffee and stirred it slowly. "You know," she told him thoughtfully, "it's not that easy. One minute you're charming, the next you're infuriating, the next you're apologizing. Maybe that's all right for you, but it's not for me. There are a lot of real differences between us. We have entirely different philosophies of life—"

"You can't possibly know that," Jack protested.

"I know how you behave," Susan said stoutly.

"I know how you behave, too," Jack said softly, leaning forward to cup her chin in his hands. He stroked her jaw, and even her headache couldn't dim the tingling his fingertips left in their wake. "Last night you behaved very nicely," he offered gently. "Like a house afire. Like a rocket."

"I don't want to discuss last night," she told him. "It was a momentary aberration. I was upset. I wasn't behaving like myself."

"Oh, I wouldn't say that," Jack challenged. "I'd say it was one of the few times you *were* behaving like yourself—in our acquaintance, that is."

Susan brushed his hand away and huddled over her coffee. "That's my point," she told him. "I tell you what I think, what I feel, and you immediately decide I don't know what I'm talking about. You always think I don't know what I'm talking about or what I'm doing. It's not just one little incident on a mountain."

Jack sat back, thoughtfully stroking his own chin rather than hers. "Maybe we just got off on the wrong foot," he suggested. "Maybe it's something we could work out."

"I don't think so," Susan said stubbornly, though the

part of her that wasn't aching was jumping with hope. She willed the rebellious emotion down. "We're just two very different personalities," she continued. "We weren't destined to get along."

"Hmm," Jack murmured pensively, seeming to study her. He stood up and began pacing slowly across the kitchen. "The thing is," he said, "whether or not we get along isn't the point here, is it? The main point is the climb."

"That wasn't what you were talking about a minute ago," Susan pointed out.

"No, it wasn't," Jack agreed. "But think of it this way. I have a climb I want to make. You want to make it, too, no matter what you think about me or our chances for amicable relations. True?"

Susan nodded. It was more than true. Whenever she let herself think about the climb independently of Jack, she felt an immediate surge of excitement and longing. A voice inside reminded her that she felt the same way whenever she thought about Jack himself, but she ignored it. That wasn't the issue here.

"I haven't climbed anything major in a long time," she sighed. "I've almost forgotten what it feels like."

Jack grinned. "Good," he said. "Now, think about this morning. Maybe I was a little precipitous, asking your assistant to bring my suitcase up here right away—"

"*Precipitous* isn't the word I'd use for it," Susan said dryly.

"How about *incorrigible?*" Jack countered easily. "The point is, there's a climb we both want to make and that would be good for both of us professionally. It would be even better if we housed the crew here at the school."

"You mean, you'd live here?" Susan asked. "All of you?"

"Of course," Jack replied. "Live here and train here."

Susan felt a shiver go up her spine. Having the crew live and train at the chalet meant having Jack there, too—twenty-four hours a day, seven days a week, maybe for months. The idea gave her an oddly queasy, excited feeling she wasn't ready to explore. After all, she'd made up her mind about her relationship with Jack. He was too arrogant, too convinced of his own superiority and her incompetence for her to have anything to do with him. If she'd had doubts about that before, that scene in her office this morning should have convinced her. But then . . .

"I don't think there would be enough room to house an entire crew," she said cautiously, wishing she could banish the niggling doubts that had begun to surface. The fact was, some of what Jack was saying made a certain amount of sense. Having the crew housed together at the school would bring much-needed publicity to her enterprise, as would her participation in a major climb. If only she could force herself to get along with Jack somehow.

She shook her head, sure that if there was some way they could force themselves to get along, they'd be concentrating on something quite other than mountain climbing. The spark that had leaped between them hadn't been doused by angry words or her reluctance. What was worse, the prospect excited her. In the intensity of that excitement she saw the extent of her danger.

"We just don't get along," she told Jack. "It keeps coming back to that."

"But we agree on the climb," Jack pointed out, smiling. "It would be good for both of us."

"I don't think you could find two climbers who wouldn't agree that making a climb no one else had ever made was good for them," she said wryly. "Doing something no one else had ever done was the impetus behind the founding of this sport."

Jack spread his hands as if to say *There now, I've made my point*. "Since we both want to make this climb," he ventured, "maybe we should *make* ourselves get along."

"How?" she asked suspiciously. "If you think I'm going to allow a repeat of last night—"

Jack shook his head. "No repeats," he promised. "Just conversation. On neutral ground."

"What would you call neutral ground?"

"Dinner," Jack promptly replied. "Seven-thirty."

"But—" Susan began. She stopped. Jack was standing with his feet apart and his arms crossed over his chest, grinning. His whole aspect made her suspicious. She knew she ought to turn him down, or at least insist on making "neutral ground" something like the lobby of the local library. This whole setup was just a little too convenient.

She asked herself what it was convenient for and couldn't come up with an answer. Then she thought of the Maidenhorn and sighed.

"All right," she told him. "But it isn't going to work."

Chapter 5

"YOU MEAN HE stayed all night?" Janie Dean exclaimed later that afternoon. "But, Susan," she enthused, "that's wonderful!"

Susan burrowed deeper into her bedroom closet and tried to concentrate on finding her other blue argyle sock. Jack's raw-egg concoction and a long nap had cured most of her hangover, but she didn't think anything was capable of curing the mixture of apprehension and excitement that had resulted from their morning talk.

She knew she was a little disorganized—the good Lord only knew what had happened to that sock—but she had never suspected that she was downright irrational. The situation simply called for her to decide between her desire for Jack and the pain giving in to that desire would inevitably cause—a decision, she told herself repeatedly, that should be easy to make. Not only was she unable to make it, however, she was incapable of even thinking about it consistently. Somehow her thoughts kept returning to the way his fingers had felt as they caressed her throat, the way his lips had felt as they parted hers. When that happened, she just stopped thinking, period. Her body's response was much too strong, much too violent, to be denied.

Now she backed out of the closet, took the still lonely blue argyle sock from where she had left it on the bed, and threw it to the carpet in disgust.

"I know there were two of them," she told Janie stubbornly. "I matched them all up when I brought up the wash."

"Maybe the mate's in the pantry," Janie said dryly. "You know, filed between anchovies and asparagus."

Susan glared at her and headed back for the closet. "I'll wear the black ones," she said. "I saw both of those just a minute ago."

"Why don't you wear a dress?" Janie suggested.

Susan sighed and started sifting through the jumbled piles of clothes in the built-in drawers at the back of the closet for the black kneesocks. Soon after Susan awakened from her nap, Janie had come up, full of legitimate business questions. But now she didn't seem interested in pursuing them. Clearly, what she wanted to talk about was Susan-and-Jack.

"No one dresses up to go out in Bresson in the season," Susan said carefully. "Except to Claire Holloway's. If I meet him at the door looking like the sweetheart of Sigma Chi, he's going to think I want—well, you know what he's going to think I want."

"So what?" Janie demanded in exasperation. "That *is* what you want, isn't it?"

Susan grabbed the black kneesocks and turned to give her young assistant a glare. It was bad enough that she couldn't control herself; she shouldn't let Janie get out of hand as well. For all her confusion, she was still sensible enough to realize that anything that happened between herself and Jack Cameron should proceed slowly, if at all. Allowing Janie to give rein to her romantic extravagances would do nothing to further that end.

"In case you hadn't noticed," she told Janie, "I'm not in the habit of jumping into bed—if that's what you're implying—with men I hardly know. Also—"

"Also nothing," Janie interrupted with a derisive hoot. "You just want to hold it against him because he yelled at you yesterday on the mountain. You always find something to hold against them."

"Which is supposed to mean what?" Susan demanded.

"Which is supposed to mean that every man isn't Dan," Janie said patiently. "Especially not this man. I've been picking up the gossip in the village, Susan. There's a lot of it, all of it favorable on the subject of Mr. John Randolph Cameron. He isn't just a hunk, you know. He's a crusader—and he's always been a very vocal defender of female climbers. You know what Jeanne St. Cloud told me?" Janie named one of the best French female mountaineers. "She said Cameron trained the woman who guided the first all-female expedition up Everest—and backed it with his own money when they couldn't get enough from the usual sources."

"Where did you see Jeanne St. Cloud?" Susan asked suspiciously.

"She's staying at the Hotel Bresson, same as Jack, same as me," Janie said. "And same as about four other oddities: Mark Henreid, Otto Freer, Marie Marten, Wolf Meinhart. I think they're here for that expedition Jack's planning."

"So it's a good crew," Susan said, shrugging. "So what? It doesn't change the fact that no matter how liberal Jack Cameron may be on the subject of female climbers, he isn't on the subject of me. He thinks I'm a complete incompetent, Janie, and not only about mountain climbing. This morning he barged into my office—"

"So it was him!" Janie exclaimed. "I've spent the whole morning thinking it was some kind of miracle. I thought you'd gotten religion or something. I might have guessed."

"He had no right to go through my papers," Susan insisted, the remembered grievance making her anger and annoyance surface once again. "He had no right to lecture me on how I conduct my business. And he certainly had no right to imply that I was a scatterbrained idiot who was completely incapable of running her own life."

"Oh, for goodness' sake!" Janie exclaimed, obviously annoyed. "Here's this perfectly beautiful man who's offering you a great expedition and a wonderful chance at romance—"

"He hasn't offered me anything of the sort!" Susan protested.

"Of course he has," Janie said blandly. "I can see it in your face. And even if I couldn't, I'd know something was up. You've started dressing three hours before he's supposed to arrive!"

"I am not—" Susan began.

Janie waved her protest away. "Rationalize it all you want," she said, "but I've been watching you. You run fifty miles an hour in the opposite direction every time a man comes near you, and then you blame it on *his* attitudes. You pull a lot of damn-fool stunts—don't interrupt me," she warned. "I may not be a mountain climber, but I'm a pretty good listener, and the general consensus is that you take too many chances. But if anybody, especially any man, tells you so, you start insisting he doesn't think you're competent. Competent! What has it got to do with competence?"

Susan pursed her mouth. "Try alpine climbing sometime," she suggested bitterly. "Then tell me the attitude of male climbers is all warmhearted concern, which you seem to think now. It eats away at you, you know. It eats away at your confidence and your spirit. And one morning you wake up—"

"We've been through all that," Janie interrupted calmly. "I'm not talking about Dan here. I'm talking about you. And what I'm telling you is that for someone with a reputation for fearlessness, you're one of the biggest cowards I've ever met."

"Don't you ever—" Susan began.

"Oh, I'll do anything I want," Janie said. "You're not going to fire me. You don't know where I put the ankle weights." She got off the bed and smoothed out the wrinkles in her skirt. "Just be careful," she warned. "If you go on this way, you're going to end up lonely and embittered."

A moment later she had disappeared out the door, leaving Susan staring after her with equal amounts of affection and exasperation. Having Janie worrying about her gave her a warm glow, but it didn't change the fact that the girl just didn't understand. To Janie, Susan's entire problem with Jack was a figment of Susan's imagination, nothing more.

Well, it was much more serious than that, Susan told herself as she folded the black kneesocks and put them aside. When Jack wasn't actively annoying her, she found the gravity of the situation hard to remember, but it didn't take much for all her fears and doubts and anger to reappear.

Jack said they could work that out, learn to get along with each other, and although she didn't really believe it, she had agreed to give it a try. She wasn't as rigid as Janie thought she was. She was attracted to Jack. More importantly, she reminded herself, she was attracted to this climb. She had to give that a chance, at least.

What she didn't have to give a chance was Jack's—and now Janie's—idea of what her ultimate relationship with Jack should be. That, she was sure, would be a disastrous experiment. To let a man who had to work at treating her as a competent equal get too close might very well destroy her, as it had almost destroyed her in her marriage to Dan.

She took a black sweater from the jumble in the second drawer and laid it out on the bed. It was about as flattering as a sack, but she didn't care. If anything could bring home to Jack just how determined she was to keep their relationship on a professional level, that sweater would do it.

And she did want to keep their relationship on a professional level, didn't she?

She was still debating the question three hours later. The black sweater was spread on the bed beside a softer, sleeker Fair Isle. Nothing she could do could make her decide between them.

Then the doorbell rang, and Susan grabbed the nearest sweater and bolted for the stairs. She was almost halfway down before she realized she was holding the Fair Isle. She slipped it over her head and arrived at the door breathless and tense, unsure if her agitation was caused by exertion or anticipation.

Her first reaction to the sight of Jack on her doorstep was relief. He was dressed in strictly professional gear—from hiking boots to canvas belt to lightweight nylon windbreaker—not a suit, as she'd feared. At least they'd match, she thought. Something told her that was a most peculiar thought to have, but she hadn't the time to examine it.

She stepped back to let him inside, and as she did so she felt a wave of uncertainty wash over her. Now what was she supposed to do with him? she wondered. How did you start "learning to get along" with someone?

Jack didn't seem inclined to say anything. He stood in her entrance hall, his long, muscular legs a little apart, his hands in his pockets, smiling down at her, waiting.

"I ought to do something you can yell at me for," Susan said nervously. "Maybe then you'd say something."

Jack laughed, a rich, deep, full-throated laugh that seemed to fill the small chalet to bursting. "Touché," he agreed, taking her hand. "I should have said hello." He leaned down and brushed her fingers with his lips. "How's that for making amends?" he inquired.

"Just fine." Susan laughed edgily, pulling her hand away to stop it from tingling. "For a minute there, I thought our 'conversation' was going to have to be telepathic."

"I do tend to keep my mouth shut," Jack admitted ruefully, making no further move in her direction. "It's all that time I spent in Nepal. The Sherpas don't talk much."

"That must have been very comfortable for you," she teased. Then she stared at the floor. She couldn't think of another thing to say. She wasn't sure if there was another thing *to* say.

When Jack didn't say anything either, Susan cleared her throat and said, "Well," in her brightest voice. It didn't work. Jack just stood there staring at her. Susan bit her lip in agitation. Maybe her half joke hadn't been a joke at all. Maybe they didn't have anything to say to each other when they weren't fighting.

Unable to stand another minute of tension, she turned toward the closet. "Just have to get my coat," she mumbled. "I mean, if we're going out—"

"Wait!"

Jack's tone was so commanding that Susan stopped almost instantly. His expression was grim. Susan found herself close to shaking with anxiety. What was wrong with him? Was he going to tell her he'd changed his mind? That he didn't want her on this expedition after all? The idea was more disturbing than she would have expected.

He leaned down and grasped her shoulders.

"I just want to ask you one question," he said solemnly. Then the corners of his mouth tilted, his eyes lit up, and he broke into a broad grin. "Aren't we being a little ridiculous?" he demanded cheerfully.

It took Susan a moment to regain her equilibrium, but when she did, her response was definitive.

She burst out laughing.

After that, it was easy. There was one tense moment in the driveway of the chalet, when Susan's slick-soled shoes hit a patch of ice and almost sent her flying. Jack seemed about to say something, but he caught himself. Instead of hearing a lecture, Susan found herself briefly steadied against Jack's arm, then free to make her own way to the car waiting in the drive. She was mollified by his restraint and pleased that his only suggestion was that she let him know where she wanted to go for dinner.

"If you're so rich you can back an expedition by yourself," she told him, "you can afford to take me to the Wienhaus."

Jack raised his eyebrows. "In these clothes? You're sure they'll let us in?"

"They're used to climbers in Bresson," Susan assured him. "They won't mind."

"Wienhaus it is," Jack acquiesced. "At least the food's supposed to be good."

* * *

The food *was* good, and nothing about the ancient, fussy decor of the restaurant could detract from it. The Wienhaus, Susan remarked to Jack, was typically Swiss— so clean you could do an appendectomy on the floor, and so cluttered you knew the maids must be getting ulcers keeping it clean. It sometimes seemed that the Swiss had never heard of plain moldings, never mind the less-is-more school of architecture that held sway everywhere else. Every mantel and lintel was carved into precious scenes of ersatz mountain life. Happy, cherub-faced yodelers grinned from the corners of the ceilings. Plump Swiss maidens offered their butter churns for inspection from the bases of salt shakers. Porcelain dolls marched across shelves built into every conceivable excuse for wall space.

"And the thing is," Susan concluded as she attacked the nearly foot-high concoction of chocolate and whipped cream she had ordered for dessert, "you just know that if you moved anything, even in all this clutter, the Swiss would immediately know it was out of place and move it back."

"Probably," Jack laughed. "What I can't understand is how anybody as, uh, disorganized as you are ever ended up in Switzerland. It's such an orderly country."

Susan gave him a suspicious glance, wondering if he was about to start carping again, but his expression was so friendly and open she relaxed.

"I wanted to be in the Alps," she told him. "When I got divorced—"

"You were married?" he asked in surprise.

Susan nodded. "Right out of college," she said, making an effort to play down her marriage. "To a boy I'd known all my life—since I was in kindergarten. Unfortunately"—she smiled—"he wasn't a mountain climber."

Jack smiled back at her, but his eyes seemed to darken

with seriousness. "I thought mountain climbers made bad risks, in your opinion. At least in personal relationships."

He looked so concerned he almost broke the light mood. Susan stared down at her dessert. It had been a wonderful dinner. She had even begun to think there might be some merit in his proposal that they learn to get along. Talking about Dan, she was sure, would only ruin their new rapport. The subject always upset her.

"I had ten thousand dollars," she told him, changing the subject, "which was my share of my mother's estate. I was free, and I wanted to climb. I'd been thinking about a climbing school for women for a long time, so—"

"So you just came and did it," Jack said approvingly. "Decisiveness. It's a good trait."

Susan laughed. "I wish I were as decisive as I appear," she confided. "Frankly, I was so frightened when I started out, I could hardly think straight. But I didn't have anything to go back to in Wyoming, and I had managed to get myself to Bresson, so I was stuck. Which was just as well, I guess."

"You've never regretted it?" Jack asked. "You don't miss marriage? You don't want to go back to the States someday, have children, that sort of thing?"

Susan stared into Jack's troubled eyes. This new line of questioning was unsettling, and he seemed intent on pursuing it. Susan's first impulse was to distrust his motives and rally her defenses, but Jack looked so honestly caring she couldn't quite bring herself to fight him. Besides, what ulterior motive could he possibly have for asking these things? He was just trying to get to know her.

She shook off the feeling that it was she who should be trying to learn more about him, and tried to frame an answer.

"I don't think I could ever give up climbing," she told him.

Jack shook his head impatiently. "Of course you couldn't give up climbing," he said. "That isn't what I asked you."

"It comes down to the same thing." Susan shrugged. "Men don't like their wives to be too . . . out of control, maybe. They want someone to stay home and be a good little wife. And mountain climbing doesn't fit into that picture very well."

Jack's eyes narrowed. "Is that what it was with your ex-husband?" he asked. "He made you choose between climbing and marriage?"

"Not exactly," Susan said, feeling increasingly agitated. "I mean, yes, in a way. But that wasn't why—"

"What was why?"

Susan flushed. "I really don't want to talk about this," she said slowly. "We've had a very pleasant time so far, and—"

"And you think this might ruin it." Jack nodded, settling back in his seat. Susan was surprised to see how relaxed he was. Only a moment before he had exuded a distinct air of tension. The change unsettled her even more than his abrupt questioning had.

"I thought we were going to talk about the climb," she ventured.

"I thought we were going to go out on the town," Jack replied easily. "See each other in a different atmosphere. Soothe the savage breast."

Susan wrinkled her nose. "The only savage breast that needs soothing around here is yours. It's full of over-protective mother-hen-ism," she said tartly.

"Oh?" Jack laughed. "As far as I'm concerned, the only savage breast that needs soothing around here is yours, with your constant death wish. Your physical *and* professional death wish, I should clarify, now that I've seen your office."

He shook his head with an exaggerated air of remorse. "Talking is obviously getting us nowhere," he said mournfully. "So why don't we try something else?" He leaned forward and took her hand in his, gently rubbing his thumb along the hollow of her palm. Susan left her hand there for a few seconds, hypnotized by its tingling. Then she pulled back, disturbed. Why did she find it so hard to keep her wits about her when Jack touched her? Only ten minutes ago she'd been congratulating herself on keeping their discussion on a cool, platonic level.

"If we're going to have a night on the town," she reminded him a little shakily, "we should keep in mind that most of this particular town closes at midnight."

Jack sighed. "I suppose that means we ought to hit the discotheques," he admitted. "But to tell you the truth, I think a Swiss discotheque must be a contradiction in terms."

"Oh, it is," Susan told him. "We've got the only orderly discotheques in the world. But we're fond of them."

At the moment she was more fond of them than Jack could know. Discotheques meant light, noise, people— hardly the ideal setting for the kind of low-key sexual challenge Jack was so fond of subjecting her to.

When they left the Wienhaus, it was snowing. Susan stopped just outside the door while Jack struggled with his coat in the entryway. The night sky was dense and opaque-looking, though bright pinpricks of starlight twinkled through a few breaks in the clouds. The night sky of Switzerland usually looked like a highly polished opal, Susan thought. Then she turned to face the most majestic of mountains and looked out over the stately march of the Alps. Like the Swiss, the Alps seemed committed to order. But unlike things Swiss, that order was only a charade. Up close, the mountains were as wild and terrifying as a hostile jungle beast—and every bit as dangerous.

"It's their dangers that make them beautiful," Susan murmured to herself. The sight of those barren, jagged peaks always left her rapt in wonder at the great convulsion of the earth that had created them. She felt the light touch of a hand on her shoulder and looked up into Jack's serious, gentle eyes.

"You've got it backward," he told her softly. "It's their beauty that makes them dangerous."

Susan wrinkled her nose. "Somehow that's exactly the kind of unexpected thing I'd expect from you," she complained. She frowned. "I don't think I put that very coherently."

Jack laughed. "Maybe it isn't a coherent experience," he suggested. "Would you like to go for a walk? I don't think either of us is in the mood for discotheques."

Susan looked up into a sky from which even the pinpricks of starlight had disappeared behind massive clouds. "I'm not usually one for discotheques," she confessed. "On the other hand, there isn't much else to do in Bresson. Without the tourists, the village has a population of about eighty-six."

"You must be exaggerating," Jack protested.

"Not at all." Susan started to walk down the drive, away from the warm light of the Wienhaus door. "This is a herding village—or it was before skiing and mountain climbing became so popular. We're always talking about the great history of climbing, but we forget that even a hundred years ago most people thought mountain climbing was a psychotic disturbance thankfully restricted to about half a dozen members of the British aristocracy."

"And some people still do?" Jack teased.

Susan crammed her hands deep into her pockets, considering. "Some people," she said with sudden conviction, "are afraid of *living*."

"Susan . . ." Jack said tentatively, his arm encircling her shoulders, his voice low and hoarse.

Susan broke away from him and walked quickly toward a steep incline at the side of the drive. Something about the combination of Jack's presence and the grandeur of the mountains was making her feel edgy and exhilarated at once, and she knew of only one thing that could relieve the tension.

"Come on," she said urgently. "I know a place."

Jack padded up behind her. "There might be a blizzard," he said anxiously. "We shouldn't be climbing."

"I keep telling you I'm not a complete idiot," she retorted. "We're not going to climb."

She found a break in the low evergreen hedge that surrounded the Wienhaus and knelt to crawl through it. When she got to the other side the stood up and looked back, asking, "Is that too small for you?"

Jack pulled himself through and stood up. "No, but what are we doing?"

"This." Susan pointed to a narrow path that seemed to materialize out of nothing on the edge of the slope. "If you don't come through that hedge, you have to climb. Usually I climb."

"By yourself," Jack said, his disapproval obvious.

Susan refused to hear the critical note. Even from here the view was breathtaking. The path wound around the edge of a small foothill that was so termed only because it began its ascent from a plateau—which was over a mile high—and therefore didn't have enough of a height-from-base to qualify as an alp. It was actually higher than many of the mountains around it, and from its side could be seen the whole panoply of the southern Alps as they wound their way to Italy.

To look out on that demonstration of natural majesty was to be apprised not of human insignificance, but of humanity's participation in an order so all-encompassing it seemed to constitute proof of the existence of God. Susan felt it as love and peace: love for a world that contained such perfection; peace because in the mountains her daily fears and annoyances dissolved and her mind and heart became quiet and full.

When she reached the end of the path, she put her hands up along the rock outcrop above her and felt for the opening. When she found it, she rubbed vigorously to melt the thin ice, then braced herself and began pulling upward.

"Think of it as a sideways chin-up," she told Jack. "When you get up and through the opening, you've got to swing until you're sitting on the ledge."

She suited action to words. In no time at all she was looking down at her favorite view of the Alps.

"I haven't done chin-ups in ten years," Jack panted as he emerged beside her. "What's—"

Susan allowed herself a small smile of satisfaction. "The point" was obvious even to cautious, critical Jack. To one side the tiny village of Bresson huddled in the hollow of the valley, looking like a winter scene in a child's snow-bubble toy. To the other side, the Alps seemed to explode in the black night air.

"Dear Lord," Jack murmured, clearly stunned. "I don't think I've ever seen anything like it."

"Not even in Nepal?" Susan teased. "Not even in the Himalayas?"

"To climbers there it's *Himalaya,* not *the Himalayas,*" Jack said absently, not taking his gaze from the scene. "And no, I've never found a place with quite this effect. Not even there."

Susan found herself a perch and sat, hugging her knees to her chest.

"This is why I came to Bresson, instead of somewhere else in Switzerland," she said, trying to keep her tone light. It wouldn't stay light, and she knew it. She'd known from the moment she'd begun leading Jack here that the romantic intimacy of the spot would ensure that whatever conversation they had would be anything but light. Right now she didn't want to think about why she'd brought him here in the first place.

"When I first came to Europe I thought I'd settle in Basel," she said, remembering. "It's a good-sized city, as Swiss cities go. It's got a large English-speaking population and an even larger one of very rich people. Unfortunately, it's also expensive. When I found out it was too expensive to live there, I started looking around. I came to Bresson, put up at the hotel, took one look at the village, and decided it was too small. And then I found this." Her hand swept out to include the scene before them.

"A place for people who aren't afraid of living?" Jack prodded.

Susan looked at him speculatively. He had, she thought, just the larger-than-lifesize perfection she loved in the mountains. With his massive arms and broad, powerful chest, his tapering waist and infinite legs, he could have been the spirit of the Alps come to life.

"I've learned a lot from the Swiss," she ruminated. "I used to wonder how my ex-husband could have been brought up in the mountains and still be so—so frightened of everything. So manipulative and controlling." She shivered in the night air, remembering. "Dan was the kind of person who needed to have everything running like clockwork. Even his wife."

"And the Swiss?" Jack asked. "They also need everything running like clockwork?"

Susan nodded. "It's as if the sight of all this untamable wildness causes a fear..." She tugged fretfully at her hair, searching for words. "I don't know if I can explain it. It's as if, since they can't control the mountains, they have to control everything else."

Jack looked skeptical. "Aren't you overgeneralizing from a single personal experience?"

Susan dislodged a pebble from the snow-covered slope and sent it bouncing down the mountainside, its path chartered for them by the series of echoes that rose from below.

"I met Dan Fraser when I was three years old," she said slowly. "I think I loved him all my life. I had every reason to think he loved me. I knew there were problems, of course. I thought we'd balance each other out. I'd bring a little excitement into his life—Dan was always a very orderly person—and he'd bring a little stability into mine. I really wanted a traditional marriage. My mother died when I was very young, and although my dad was wonderful, there was only so much he could do. I suppose I thought... I don't know what I thought."

Jack rose from his rocky perch and came to sit beside her. He leaned against her, and his arm claimed her shoulder once again.

"How old were you?" he asked her gently. "When you married?"

"Twenty-one," Susan said tightly.

Jack stroked her hair. "Don't you realize you were probably just too young? Twenty-one is too soon to know what kind of a person you are. If you made a mistake—"

"I made a mistake all right," Susan agreed bitterly. "Only it wasn't the kind of person *I* am that was the problem. Oh, I caused my share of the trouble between us. I couldn't give up climbing, and I couldn't stop myself from being affected by the way Dan attacked me for it. I resented the way he needled me. He kept harping about 'being careful, taking care,' and it sapped my confidence. It made me feel uneasy and afraid and clumsy, and sometimes I was ready to kill him for it. But I was willing to try to work that through. That wasn't what broke us up."

"What was?" Jack probed.

Susan wondered where to start and whether she could ever explain. "Dan wanted a perfect corporate wife," she said. "He wanted me to give parties and smile at his boss and wear perfectly prim little pastel dresses to all the right places. He thought it was important for his career, and I accepted that. I wanted him to succeed. He thought that my climbing was bad for his image, and he wanted me to stop. So I tried. I really tried. Only it didn't work."

"I know how that is," Jack sighed. "Once I spent a whole season laid up with mononucleosis. By the end of the second week off the mountains, I was crazy enough to eat the wallpaper."

Susan smiled in spite of herself. "I was crazier than that," she said. "I took all the plates out of the china closet and smashed them. When Dan came home we had a terrible fight. Then he walked out—permanently. Three weeks later, before I'd even filed for divorce, he was engaged to a secretary at his office. It was unofficial, of course, but that didn't make it any less real. I suspect Dan thought of women the way most people think of cars. If one breaks down and you can't fix it, you go out and buy one that works."

"Susan." Jack's hand came up to cup and caress the

nape of her neck. "You can't tell me every man in the world is looking for a robot to fit his preconceived idea of perfection. You must know that isn't true."

"I know," Susan sighed. "Dan was an extreme case. If I hadn't been so blinded by love, so in need of something steady and permanent in my life, I'd probably have seen that sooner."

"Then what is it?" Jack insisted.

"What it is"—Susan threw another pebble down the mountain—"is climbing. Dan wasn't any different from most men in that respect, you know. Men don't like their women climbing. It's dangerous. And whether the intentions are honorable concern or sly manipulativeness, the results are the same. First comes all that harping on safety, which I know from experience only undermines my self-confidence. Then comes disaster. Maybe there's a man out there who's capable of taking what I do for a living in stride, but I haven't met him yet."

For a moment they were silent, Susan's oddly emphasized *yet* hanging in the night between them. She felt drained. Even the mountains couldn't lift her spirits now. Thinking about Dan always made her weary and edgy.

She rubbed the cold surface of her cheek against Jack's ungloved hand. It was warm and slightly chapped, its back covered with fine hairs that felt like down against her skin. There was something so relaxing about it, as if *this* man could smooth away the pain that had been etched into her heart by the betrayal of the other.

He slid his hand down and grasped her shoulder, turning her until she was facing him. His eyes held an infinity of compassion. Staring into them, Susan found herself desperately wishing for the amnesia she'd need before she could lose herself in their depths.

"Part of me wants to go out and kill your ex-husband," Jack said ruefully. "But part of me"—here he traced a pattern across her forehead with his fingertips—"part of me wants to shake you, to force you to understand that it doesn't have to be the way you think it does. Concern doesn't have to be debilitating, Susan, and it doesn't have to be manipulative. You can have love and climbing, too, if you aren't afraid to take it."

Susan turned away. "I lived with one man who didn't think I was a competent climber," she said tightly. "A man who thought I was going to get hurt whenever I left the house in anything but high heels. It took me nearly three years after the divorce to feel like myself again. I can't go through something like that twice."

"You don't have to." He turned her to face him again. "You've only known me a couple of days. You've decided I think you're incompetent. You've decided my concern means the same thing your ex-husband's did, that's it's only a subtle way of denigrating you. You can't know that, because it isn't true. And even if it were, it would be much too early to tell."

"If it's much too early for me to tell," Susan choked out, "then it's much too early for you to be talking about love."

"Is it?" Jack whispered softly, his eyes darkening to deeply mysterious pools. "Love isn't a jigsaw puzzle, Susan. It's never too early to tell."

Susan knew even before he bent his head what would happen next. She didn't try to stop it. She was fascinated by his lips, by the taut muscles of his jaw, by the hooded, insistent probing of his eyes. Her lips were parted when he reached her. Her arms went automatically, willingly, around his neck as he pulled her close against him. She didn't protest when she felt him unzipping first his jacket and then her own. She wanted to be as close to him as it was possible to be in this cold and barren place where they found themselves alone and drawn to each other.

She wanted to forget her resolutions and her past, and to bask for a few brief moments in overwhelming sensation.

It was a gentle kiss, but a dangerously promising one. His hot tongue darted and probed into the recesses of her mouth as his large hands stroked first her neck, then her shoulders, then moved lightly over the soft wool of her sweater where it covered her breasts. With warmth flooding through every molecule of her bones and nerves and skin, Susan twisted and turned under his caresses, wishing she could fuse with Jack into one body, one soul, one heart.

It seemed to be all the encouragement he needed. His tentative, seductive forays became more urgent, and with one hand at the small of her back holding her firmly against his massive chest, he slid the other up under her sweater, his fingers splaying over her ribcage, dipping to tease her naval, and returning to cup her breast. She surged into his embrace, and his tantalizing hands left her just long enough to lock her arms more securely around his neck. She heard herself whimper faintly as the warmth of his skin was replaced by the roughness of his sweater, but then his fingers were back at her breasts, encompassing them, the sheer size of his hands making her feel tiny and delicate and infinitely cherished.

"With love you can always tell," he whispered hoarsely. "From the beginning, you can always tell."

He pressed his lips against the base of her throat. His tongue explored the sensitive hollow there, making her flame with a desire so violent she didn't think it could ever be satisfied, leaving her with the knowledge that in those fleeting moments she was fully alive, fully aware, fully a woman.

Their lips met again, insistently, conpulsively, and when they reluctantly broke apart for breath, Susan resented the cold air that rushed to fill the space between them. She wanted to return to the comfort of Jack's embrace, and to its promise. She wanted to hide herself against him and forget the things she knew would now begin to crowd her thoughts and tear her away from him.

But the cold seemed to bring Jack to his senses, and the mood between them shifted subtly. His hands left her breasts and straightened her sweater, and he stroked her face, sending out electric signals that made Susan shudder.

"I keep telling myself I have to go slowly," he murmured ruefully, "but I don't know how slowly I can go. Every time I see you, all I can think about is holding you in my arms, cherishing you, loving you."

"Even that first time on the mountain yesterday?" Susan asked him with a tremor in her voice.

"Especially that first time on the mountain." He slipped his arms around her waist and locked his hands against the small of her back. "I thought you were the most beautiful woman I'd ever seen. Then when you started fighting with me, telling me off—I didn't agree with what you were saying, but I respected you for being able to say it. You were magnificent."

"What am I supposed to say to that?" Susan asked helplessly, blushing in spite of herself. "No one's ever called me magnificent before."

Jack smiled and nuzzled her hair. "Say you'll climb with me," he coaxed. "We could be so good together, on a mountain and off. We could help each other professionally and explore what's happening between us at the same time. Especially the exploring." He paused. "And you know as well as I do that it isn't just sex, Susan."

"I know," she sighed. She abruptly pulled out of his grasp, stood, then began to fumble with the zipper of her jacket. Suddenly she wanted the protective shell of nylon close around her.

"Maybe I can see the exploring," she told him nervously. "When I make myself stop thinking, I can see it all too well. Of course I'm attracted to you. That's never been an issue. But the climb!" She shook her head. "Don't you realize," she pleaded with him, "the climb is the whole point. I know you don't take me seriously when I say I couldn't bear to work with you if you behaved the way you did yesterday on the mountain—"

"Of course I take you seriously," Jack interrupted. "I'll always take you seriously."

"Then take this seriously," Susan insisted. "If we're going to explore those possibilities you keep mentioning, what I need from you is your professional respect and support, your acceptance of me as an equal. If that's missing, the only possible outcome is catastrophe. I know we're attracted to each other, Jack. I'm not going to be willing or able to take that any further than it's already gone unless I also know you can meet my conditions."

"And how do you expect to do that?" Jack asked calmly. "If you refuse to climb with me, how am I supposed to prove I'm not secretly considering you a total incompetent?"

Susan looked down at him uncertainly. "I'm not sure," she said uneasily, realizing that he had a point. "Time, I suppose."

"And where are we supposed to get the time?" Jack quizzed. He got to his feet, clutching at his jacket zipper. "We both have work to do," he said. "On the slopes and off. If we're not involved in a common enterprise, when are we going to have time to see each other?"

"But you're talking about a major expedition!" Susan protested. "We'd be spending weeks living in the same house, seeing each other every day. Things would escalate, Jack. You know they would. And right now, as far as I can tell, you're worse than a bad risk."

Jack frowned, seeming to consider her objections. Sticking his hands deep into his pockets, he paced almost to the edge of the small ledge where they stood. Susan had to grit her teeth to keep from warning him of the danger of falling. It would be too perfect a role reversal, she thought with humor, and she wouldn't blame him for taking full advantage of it. Fortunately, he soon turned and paced back to where she stood, well away from the precipice.

"How about this," he offered. "Tomorrow we'll get our gear, go back to where we met, and climb. Together. If I don't manage to treat you like the next best thing to a Sherpa guide, we'll call the whole thing off. If I manage to meet your stringent requirements"—his eyes gleamed—"then we set up at your chalet and we make the Maidenhorn climb together."

It was such a simple and logical solution, Susan almost didn't know what to do with it. She took a deep breath, caught herself counting to ten again, and made herself stop. It was too reasonable a request to dismiss, even though it made her distinctly uneasy. She was sure there was a loophole in his reasoning, but at the moment she couldn't find it.

Feeling suddenly reckless, she dismissed her misgivings and agreed.

"You'll have to be pretty good," she warned him, "and very careful. I'm serious about this, Jack."

"I know you are." Once again he slipped his arms around her waist, but it was a friendly gesture this time. He grinned at her. "I'll be very good," he promised. "And very, very careful."

Chapter 6

JANIE DEAN CAME early the next morning. Too early. Susan had intended being up and out long before her assistant arrived, but she'd hardly finished dressing when she heard the downstairs door slam. Damn, Susan thought irritably. Janie was never this early, especially on Sunday. The girl must be dying for news of what was going on between Susan and Jack.

Since that was exactly what Susan didn't want to discuss, the sound of Janie pattering around downstairs was anything but welcome. Susan tried to be silent as she stuffed an extra hat and pair of gloves into her day pack. The chances of escape were slim. If Janie was determined to corral her, all she had to do was sit tight and wait for Susan to come down. After that, Susan knew it would just be a matter of time before Janie's badgering forced her to reveal more than she wanted to.

She sat down on the bed and tried to think, then gave it up and admitted to herself that what she wanted was an excuse for doing something she knew was stupid. She looked guiltily toward the window. Then she glanced at her pack, where she knew her rappel rope was. Her jacket was draped over the chair that stood beside her bedroom closet, just where she'd left it last night. There were extra scarves and gloves and hats in her dresser drawers, so it didn't matter that she'd left the ones she'd worn last night on the kitchen table. The only problem was finding a secure place to tie the rope.

She jumped off the bed, grabbed her jacket from the chair, and started pawing through her dresser in search of gloves and a scarf. This whole plan was ridiculous, she knew, but she was convinced it was necessary. She'd had a long, restless night and an equally agitated morning, and she wasn't ready to face Janie's enthusiasm. She could still feel the hot promise of Jack's kiss every time she closed her eyes; just thinking about their coming climb together left her weak with anticipation and confusion.

She tied the rappel rope around the bedpost nearest the wall, then eased open the window and dropped the rope out. Since the bed was a brass antique that weighed enough to throw her back out every time she'd had to move it, she was fairly sure it would hold. What she wasn't so sure of was how to establish a stance on the slick surface of the chalet's wooden siding.

Speculation wasn't going to get her anywhere. She grabbed the rope, backed toward the window, and pushed herself into the cold, butt first, propelling her feet forward so that they, not her torso, hit the side of the chalet. She must have misjudged the coil hitch in her safety loop, because her first fall was much faster and farther than she'd expected. She experienced the sick feeling in the pit of her stomach that usually precedes disaster for mountain climbers, and the thought raced through her mind that if she fell and broke something, she'd have to sit still and listen to one of Jack's lectures. And this time he'd be right. She was pulling a damn-fool stunt, and she knew it.

Then her feet hit the siding, she bounced, and training and experience took over. In no time at all she was at the bottom, offering up a prayer of thanksgiving to Saint Bernard. All of this fuss just to avoid Janie Dean—her *employee*. What sort of state could she be in to have sunk so low?

Susan unhitched the rappel rope from her belt. She'd call Janie from the SafetyPhone at the start of the training climb and tell her to close the window and bring in the rope.

She hurried across the snow-filled yard behind the chalet, adjusting the straps of her day pack as she walked. It was delightful to be out in the cold, clear air of morning. Her sleep last night had been riddled with dreams that alternated between idyllic forays into a blissful Eden and full-scale nightmares. Apparently not even her subconscious could decide on the proper inferences to be drawn from the myriad events of the past few hectic days. She was certain only that, no matter how this new experiment of theirs turned out, Jack had changed her life forever. She would never again be as secure in her isolation as she had been just one second before she looked up from the end of a safety rope and saw that giant of a man standing on the mountain

When she reached the last rise before the path to the training climb, she stopped, searching the area for the tall, imposing form she both feared and longed to see. He was crouched on the ground over his day pack, rearranging the items inside. His hat was tucked under his arm, and the wind blew freely through his straight yellow hair.

Susan's heart lurched at the sight of him. Only a

supreme act of will allowed her to assume the mask of calm she needed to greet him with. She might not be able to sort out her feelings about Jack, but she felt no confusion at all about this particular climb. This was her chance to see if it was possible for the two of them to learn to get along, as Jack had put it. Her participation in the Maidenhorn expedition and her future relationship with Jack rested on the outcome of this morning's ascent. She was determined to do it right.

Gathering her wits, she started down the gentle slope. Jack saw her when she was halfway down, and he stood and waved, holding something in the air.

"Got an idea," he shouted up to her.

She took the rest of the hill at a trot and came to a halt beside him. "Pitons," she gasped. "What do we need pitons for? That face has enough stationaries to make a ladder."

Jack pointed to a jagged face to the west of the training climb. "Look at that," he directed. "There's a ledge about a hundred feet higher than the one on the training climb. And it isn't mapped. We'd have to figure it out ourselves." He turned to look seriously into her eyes. "I'd say this was a better test. We'd have to place pitons. We'd have to map. We're going to have to do that if we make an expedition together."

Susan nodded, trying to match his seriousness. She had to turn away from him to do it. Part of her was both annoyed and disappointed that Jack was so businesslike. There was no hint in his manner that anything intimate had happened between them last night. That, of course, was the way she'd told him she expected him to behave. Even so, she hadn't been prepared for—

Susan decided that whatever she hadn't been prepared for didn't matter, and she turned her attention to the climb he was proposing. It certainly was a more interesting route than the one she took almost every day. She turned to him and nodded. "My only objection," she told him, "is that it's a sheer face and we're at ground zero. How do we get a piton into it from here?"

Jack's face broke into a grin. "I was just thinking that myself," he said smugly, "when it occurred to me that there was more than one advantage in the fact that you're so small and I'm so tall."

Susan flushed at the wicked twinkling in his eyes, almost wishing she could return to her disappointment of a moment before. Now that she was once again subjected to his sexual challenge, she knew she didn't want him behaving that way while they were climbing.

"Concentrate on the face," she told him sternly. "What does it have to do with the fact that I'm, uh, shorter than you are?"

Jack's eyebrows quirked in amusement. "That isn't exactly what I said," he drawled, "but I suppose it'll have to do. What do you weigh, about a hundred and fifteen?"

"A hundred and ten." Susan was mystified by the question.

"I weigh about two hundred," he said, "and I've got fairly broad shoulders. Which means"—his arm traced a triumphant flourish in the air—"all you have to do is climb onto my shoulders and drive the first piton in at what will then be eye level. Once we have the first one in, we can hand to hand. We'll be a human gradation slope, or close to it."

Susan stared at him, appalled. "Good Lord!" she erupted when she managed to surmount her shock. "And you accuse *me* of being nuts! That's the craziest idea I've ever heard!"

"Why?" Jack challenged. "If you think about it, it's the safest way to place the first piton. Any of the traditional ways would leave a margin for error. If we shot the thing in, which is what all the books—including mine—tell you to do, we could hit loose rock or place on a fault, and the piton could come out. This way, you can see the placement."

"I should have known," Susan said wryly, "that even your crazy ideas would have something to do with safety."

Jack shook his head regretfully. "I never said I was against acceptable risks," he chided her. "Our arguments usually revolve around our different definitions of what's acceptable."

Susan rubbed her arms nervously. "Don't start that," she admonished him. "All we need now is to start an argument before we're even off the ground." She wandered over to the face and inspected it. "How do you know I won't fall off your shoulders?" she quizzed him.

"Trust me," Jack coaxed. "It's all a matter of balance." He knelt in the snow and patted his back. "Come on," he urged. "Sling your knees over my shoulders. After I've stood up, you can stand up. It's easy."

Susan wasn't convinced, but her sense of adventure was too strong to let her refuse. Besides, she liked being on the other end of the risk-taking stick for once. Jack's idea was crazy, but Susan liked him crazy better than she liked him overprotective.

She climbed onto his back and held tightly to his head while he got to his feet. Then, using the hands he offered as a lever, she maneuvered until she was standing on his shoulders. Then she took the piton out of her belt and leaned against the cold sheet of rock that was the mountain face.

"I like it up here," she called down. "It's got *elegance*," she added, using the traditional climber's phrase for a particularly resourceful or skillful solution to a problem.

Jack patted her foot reassuringly. "You're doing fine," he told her. "Just hammer that piton in as far as it'll go."

Susan took the hammer out of her belt. "Hang on. You've never heard hammering the way you're about to hear hammering," she promised him. Then she leaned forward and started to pound the flat-headed steel needle into the rock.

She felt totally happy. There was a boldness and daring to this scheme of Jack's that she wouldn't have thought him capable of. It offered the first concrete proof that there might be a way to resolve their differences, that there might be something in his personality that was as in love with the wild and the dangerous as she was—and he might be willing to share it.

They were halfway to the outcrop before Susan noticed something was wrong. She was mapping—moving ahead, choosing their objectives, plotting the route to those objectives, then planting the pitons. Since this was a short climb, they would leave the pitons in the side of the mountain while they ascended and remove them on their way down. Ascent-mapping was a dangerous and difficult job, usually left to the expedition leader on major climbs, and Susan knew that by giving her this job, Jack was telling her better than words ever could that he was at least trying to trust her professional capabilities. His confidence in her was as exhilarating as her discovery that, even after all this time, she could skillfully complete the delicate process. She was beginning to feel better than she had in years.

Unfortunately, she was also beginning to feel a little frustrated. She was short, and since she could reach only so far, the distance between the pitons she was planning was correspondingly small. She knew they would be moving twice as quickly if Jack was mapping. Even if they traded off they'd be able to reach the outcrop at a much faster pace.

She looped her safety rope around the piton she had just hammered into the slope and sighed. She hated giving up her position of superiority, but at the rate she was bringing them up the face it was going to take all day just to make the ascent.

She braced her feet against the loops she had made by tying long strands of one-inch flat webbing into etriers, or stirrups. Then she looked down the face for Jack. If she could get his attention, she might be able to signal him to start trading the lead with her.

She saw him two pitons below her. He was unhooking himself from a rest etrier and preparing to ascend toward her position, and for a while she couldn't make contact. Then he looked jerkily in her direction, and she caught his eye.

What she saw there nearly made her heart stop. She didn't think she'd ever in her life seen such a look of pure terror on anyone's face. Jack's features were contorted with fear. He was holding on to his safety rope as if it was the only lifeline in a situation of unavoidable disaster, and bracing himself against the mountain as if the last thing he wanted to do was move in her direction.

Susan turned quickly away, knowing he had seen her but not caring. For a moment she was numb with pain and incomprehension; then she began to feel the hot, quick flush of fury spreading through her veins. It was all a sham, then. He was being the perfect gentleman, the ultimate nonsexist equal among equals, but what was really going through his mind was the same old distrust that had so enraged her from the beginning. He didn't think of her as a competent climber. He was simply willing to endure the pain of pretending he did to get her to go along with his plans!

She held a piton to the rock above her head, took out her hammer, and pounded it with lethal fury into the face. She was going to get them to that outcrop so fast it would make Jack Cameron's head spin. She had no intention of spending any longer than she had to climbing with a man who looked like—like *that* when she was in the lead.

She pulled herself up to the new piton, webbed herself in, and concentrated on the next one up. Nothing mattered now but getting to the top as quickly as possible. She had been intending to try a traverse and a belay, just to see how she and Jack worked together in those situations, but she didn't have to bother now. She knew how they worked together.

She was at the outcrop before she realized it. She knew she should bucket-hold up—it was the kind of outcrop angle that called for that method—but she didn't have the patience. She just front-pointed and hopped, landed neatly on the ledge, and started to marshal her emotional resources. She wanted to be prepared when Jack reached her.

His head popped over the ledge as she was beginning to form the first of her indictments against him. She never had a chance to open her mouth. He was standing before her in an instant, and he was furious.

"What did you think you were doing?" he demanded of her. "This is a ninety-degree outfall. You should have been doing a bucket-hold."

Susan couldn't believe what she was hearing. "How dare you get angry at me!" she sputtered. "I could have hopscotched over that outfall, and it wouldn't have mattered a damn. But *you!*" She threw her day pack to the ground in disgust. "If that's what you call making an effort to treat me like a competent climber, I'll eat a piton!"

Jack's jaw tightened. "I let you map," he said with even but dangerous iciness. "I let you lead an ascent, for heaven's sake. What more do you want of me?"

"How about a vote of confidence?" she asked bitterly. "The look on your face could have gotten you the role of prime victim in a horror movie. There's probably less panic on the faces of men about to die in the electric chair!"

Jack's expression changed. Something resembling pain seemed to replace the anger, then disappear. He turned away and began to unload his pack.

"That had nothing to do with you," he said finally, his voice low. "I always look that way when I climb. At least that's what people tell me."

Susan didn't know what to make of that at all. "In the first place," she said, "I don't believe you. In the second, if it is true, I don't understand how you can lead expeditions. Anybody that terrified of a simple little face like this one has no business being on a mountain at all."

Jack's face set in a stubborn scowl. "If you don't believe me, you can ask Jeanne St. Cloud and the others I've worked with. They'll all tell you the same thing. And it isn't terror. I love the mountain—maybe even more than you do."

"I know terror when I see it," Susan insisted, though her voice wavered a little. "And we've been through all this. I need your confidence, Jack, and I don't have it."

"You have it." Though his eyes were still serious, he leaned over and playfully pulled her cap off her head. "Believe me, that look on my face had nothing to do with you. You were excellent down there. You have a real instinct for what will work on a face, and your etrier system was flawless. You're even better than I expected you to be."

"You didn't expect much," Susan said tartly, wanting to hold on to her anger. She couldn't. His words were honey to her. She wanted so badly to believe him it hurt.

He must have heard the hope in her voice, because he grinned at her and held out his pack. "I spent all morning preparing this," he told her. "I didn't expect to use it as a peace offering."

Susan looked down at the collection of breads, cheeses, and pâtés and nearly groaned out loud. She'd been so busy avoiding Janie Dean this morning that she hadn't had any breakfast, and she was starving.

She knew nothing was resolved between Jack and her, but she couldn't make herself continue their argument. Not only was she hungry, but she'd just remembered that she hadn't called Janie from the SafetyPhone. The thought of that rappel rope hanging from the open window of her bedroom had her cringing with embarrassment and went a long way toward making her feel more accommodating about Jack's infuriating behavior on the face. After all, she tried to tell herself, everyone tended to behave oddly in times of stress. And she had placed Jack in a test situation, thereby creating stress.

She abandoned her reasoning, and with it her anger. She reached into Jack's day pack and extracted a runny piece of Brie.

"Did you bring forks?" she asked him.

"I've got a Swiss Army knife," he offered.

"You have one of the more elaborate models, I'll bet." She grinned. "The kind with a knife and fork and everything else on it."

Jack unhooked the heavy utensil from his belt. "You could build a house with one of these," he boasted, "and then have everything you needed to move in."

Susan spread a waterproof shield on the ground and

sat down. "We still haven't resolved anything," she reminded him. "When we get to the ground, I have every intention of bringing this up again."

With one hand Jack handed her a roll spread with Brie. He tweaked her nose with the other. "When we get to the ground, you'll be convinced," he promised her.

She was not convinced. She wasn't unconvinced, either, but doubt seemed to film her every thought about the proposed expedition. It was true that Jack looked just as terrified when he was in the lead, which he was on their descent, as he had been when she led. But did that prove his fear had nothing to do with her, as he had claimed? Maybe he'd be frightened to be climbing with her under any circumstances, even when he was almost literally controlling her every movement. She had the honesty to admit that that didn't make much sense. If he was so frightened about what she might do, why would he want to climb with her at all?

She hit the ground thinking she could do nothing but agree to his scheme. The potential benefit to herself and her school was much too large to throw away on the basis of increasingly vague doubts. Every time she thought she had things figured out, Jack came up with a new twist that made everything look different. And every time she realized that turning him down would mean almost never seeing him for the rest of the winter, her heart was filled with dismay. She was getting very attached to Jack Cameron.

She unhooked the safety rope from her belt and began to coil it around her hand. She knew Jack was standing at her side, waiting expectantly for her comment, but she needed a few moments to collect her thoughts. Finally, realizing she could postpone it no longer, she dumped the rope over the hitch at the side of her day pack and said, "All right, with conditions."

Jack's face managed to both brighten and darken at once, a paradox that fascinated Susan. He ran a hand through his hair and pursed his lips. "What conditions?" he asked warily.

Susan started walking slowly down the path that would lead them to the chalet. "I promise to provide accommodations for the crew no matter what happens, but not for you. You can stay at the chalet as long as we get along, but once we start fighting, you leave. Understood?"

Jack grinned. "Oh, we'll get along," he promised. "I have every intention of ensuring that we get along very well."

"And that's another thing," Susan began.

Jack stopped her with his arms. "You can't tell me you're going to forbid that," he complained. "I don't think it would do any good anyway. I doubt you do, either."

Susan disengaged herself. "I didn't say I was going to forbid anything. But you've got to understand, I don't, I don't—" She shrugged helplessly. "Why is it so impossible to explain anything to you?" she said crossly.

"Because you're trying to explain nonsense," Jack promptly supplied. He drew her to him, his hands laced behind her back and his thighs pressed against hers. Susan shuddered involuntarily, her feelings of the night before palpably revived.

"You're creating a problem where none exists," he added softly. "You're trying to think up reasons why we shouldn't be together. But there aren't any, Susan. It's just your fear."

"I'm not afraid," she said sharply.

He answered her by leaning down for a kiss, and in

spite of her best intentions, she found herself responding to him. His nose was warm against her cold cheek. Where they touched, she felt an electric zinging that was almost a hum. She clung to his neck, reveling in the simple yet intoxicating feel of his silky hair against her wrist.

When he drew away from her at last, his eyes were kind and coaxing. He stroked her face with infinite tenderness, his light, feathery touches seeming to promise a world of excitement just on the other side of restraint.

"Of course you're afraid," he said gently. "You're afraid of being hurt again. I can understand that." He smiled wryly. "Maybe it's just as well I've never had that experience. I've dated a lot of women in my life, but I've never been as . . . attached to any of them as I'm getting to you. Maybe that's why I don't have any patience where you're concerned. I feel I have to take you fast, before you get away."

Susan nervously pulled away. "There you go again," she muttered, "turning things around. Every time I think I'm in one place, you put me in another."

Jack's eyebrows rose. "Was that supposed to make sense?" he teased.

Susan began pacing up and down the walk in exasperation. "How can you ask me to make sense?" she demanded. "You don't make sense. One day you walk into my life, two days later you want me to make several very important decisions, and you won't even give me the time to gather evidence."

"This isn't a court of law," Jack pointed out. "It's your heart I'm asking for. You have all the evidence you need for that."

"Do I?"

"You know how I feel when I hold you in my arms, Susan. You know how you feel, too. What more do you want?"

"We can't spend every moment in—in—" Susan stopped herself, appalled.

But Jack wasn't about to be put off. He scooped her into his arms again, holding her even more closely than before. Susan experienced the dizzying sense of vertigo that was the beginning of the slow flame of desire Jack could always ignite within her. That much of what he'd been saying was true. She did know how he felt when he held her—and how she felt. It was a compelling argument, almost too compelling to resist.

Almost, but not quite. Unless he was kissing her, it was difficult to forget the subject of their disputes—and the way he often seemed to regard her as an inept buffoon. The pain of those moments was the only thing stopping her from agreeing to everything he asked.

"I've agreed to climb with you," she said desperately. "I've even agreed to let you move into my house. Isn't that enough for now?"

He brushed her cheek with his lips. "For now," he agreed. "But, Susan, you've got to realize, it can't go on much longer. We're driving each other crazy."

"Right now you're driving me crazy," she admitted, disengaging herself once again. "I understand what you're saying, Jack, but you've got to give me a little time. I may seem reckless, but I'm really a very cautious person."

"Too cautious sometimes," Jack sighed. He looked regretful when she started to move down the path, but he didn't protest. Instead he fell into step beside her, his hands in his pockets, his face thoughtful.

They were in sight of the chalet when he stopped her once again. Susan vacillated, debating whether or not to ask him in. It seemed the right thing to do, but she was sure he'd see it as a new invitation to intimacy. And given the turmoil her emotions were in, she concluded she'd had enough of that for one day.

As it turned out, Jack wasn't interested in being asked in. He had other things on his mind.

"Let's look at it this way," he told her. "If we're going to make this expedition, I've got to go to Zürich for a week and set up the PR schedule. I was going to leave tonight, but maybe I'll go this afternoon and get a start on the whole process."

Susan tried to keep her disappointment from showing. Damn the man. A minute ago she'd wanted to push him away. Now she was grieving because she wouldn't be able to see him for a week.

"The crew can move in while you're gone," she suggested, keeping her tone strictly businesslike. "We'll be all set up by the time you get back."

"That's fine," Jack said blandly, "but that wasn't my point. How about this. While I'm away, you think about us—about what you need from me, about how you feel. Just don't dismiss the idea out of hand. Think about it."

I can't stop thinking about it, Susan reflected. She shook her head to clear it. She couldn't tell him that. With so bold an invitation, he'd be camped at her bedroom door before she could say boo.

"Thinking about it won't help," she countered. "It's not what I think; it's what you do. That has to change first."

"Think about it," Jack insisted. Then he smiled, changing the mood and the subject at once. "We're going to be famous," he told her brightly. "We're going to be on the first team to scale the east face of the Maidenhorn."

"Don't jinx the climb," Susan said nervously.

He laughed, then wrapped her close to him again, hugging her with playful exhilaration. "First the Maidenhorn, then Everest, then who knows? They must have mountains on the moon. When we get back we can run as the first male-female presidential–vice presidential team in history."

"I won't run unless I can be boss," Susan warned him.

"I wouldn't have it any other way," Jack agreed. Then he lowered his head. "I'm going off to the public relations wars," he said in mock seriousness. "Take something to remember me by."

Susan let him cradle her head and lifted her mouth for his kiss. She knew his touch would wipe away all her doubts, all her fears, all her memories. Right now she wanted that desperately. It was the only thing that could calm her.

She made no false promises to herself about keeping her cool during the coming week. She knew she wouldn't be able to. But no matter how often her mind warned her that she was leaving herself open to pain and bitterness and despair, she couldn't regret her moments of intimacy with Jack. Already their short time together meant more to her than anything else ever had.

Chapter 7

IF SUSAN HAD had any time to think, she might have panicked and called the whole thing off. As it was, she hardly had time to sleep.

First the crew members began appearing in search of food, lodging, and company. Janie Dean was busy during the day arranging a sleeping bag dormitory in the weight room, mapping out open areas for group training, and ordering food supplies by the gross from Bresson. Since both Jeanne St. Cloud and Marie Marten wanted to try the WACS training series, Susan added another class to her already crowded schedule.

At night she chaperoned the group around Bresson's in-season nightspots, where they showed an alarming enthusiasm for staying up until the wee hours of the morning. How they managed to rise bright and early each day and plunge happily into calisthenics was more than Susan could fathom. It must, she decided, have something to do with the fact that almost all the crew members were Europeans. From what Susan remembered, American crews were much more dedicated to sleep.

When she did have half a second to herself, Susan thought of Jack, but she was so distracted with work that her thoughts were contradictory and disconnected. On the one hand, she could hardly hear his name pronounced without feeling a stab of longing and an echo of desire. The man had affected her so strongly that he followed her into her dreams, and several mornings she woke with the unshakable conviction that her sleeping hours were being spent in the steamy embraces of a blond giant whose every touch turned her bones to jelly.

On the other hand, memories of their last climb together haunted her. The more Susan thought about the look on Jack's face as he ascended the mountain behind her, and his instinctive anger when she front-pointed the ledge, the more uncomfortable she was about the prospect of the Maidenhorn climb. Jack might think dismissing the problem would make it go away, but she knew it wasn't that easy. There was a real problem between them, and if they cared about the safety of the Maidenhorn climb, they would take pains to solve it quickly.

By the end of the week Susan was exhausted in every sense of the word. Only the knowledge that Jack was due to arrive on Sunday kept her going.

"I hope he gets here early," she told Janie on Sunday morning as she drank more coffee to stay awake. "If I don't get a nap sometime today, I'm going to go stark, raving mad."

"You do look a little peaked," Janie agreed. "I read somewhere that sleep deprivation is the most stressful ordeal a human being can experience. That's what they do to spies when they capture them. They don't let them sleep, and when they've been awake for three or four days they're so crazy they'll tell anything."

Susan shot Janie a thanks-a-lot look and went back to her coffee.

"Just keep telling yourself the school is becoming famous," Janie suggested. "That ought to keep you going."

"That's easy for you to say," Susan complained. "You go back to the hotel every night and get eight hours of unconsciousness. You sure you don't want to move in here for the duration?"

"No way," Janie said emphatically. "I like the hotel. I've got a cheap room, I've got maid service, I've got fresh rolls every morning. And"—she grinned wickedly— "I've got gossip. You want to hear the latest?"

"Not if you're going to tell me Jack Cameron is the major force behind Grandmothers' Lib, I don't," Susan said with a scowl. "Janie, where do you pick up this stuff? I've lived in Bresson for three years, and the most I can get out of anyone around here is the time of day."

"I listen," Janie said airily. Then she leaned eagerly across the table. "But this is good," she confided. "And it's not Grandmothers' Lib, either. You know C & C Sporting Goods?"

"Of course I know it," Susan said. "It's the biggest sporting equipment company in the world. It's practically a conglomerate." She had an unpleasant thought and tried to ignore it. "Don't tell me," she begged Janie.

"But I will tell you," Janie said triumphantly. "C & C—Cameron and Cameron!"

"No wonder he doesn't need a backer for this climb," Susan said wrathfully. "He's a backer himself. And he implied he was funding this expedition from the royalties of his books!"

"But he probably is!" Janie was so excited, she was jumping up and down like a child with a lollipop. "That's the good part. According to my sources—and don't look like that; my sources are my sources, and they haven't failed us yet—about five years ago, C & C was backing a race up the Matterhorn. Two teams: one male and one female."

Susan frowned. "I remember hearing about that," she said slowly. "Didn't something happen on that climb?" She searched her memory and came up with nothing. "I can't remember."

"You can't remember because there was no climb," Janie said. "Jack went to his brother and his uncle—they run the company now that his father is dead—and told them to stop it. Races aren't safe, et cetera, et cetera. They refused. So Jack went to the teams and talked them out of it. They didn't climb, and they made a big media stink about the whole race idea. Jack has hardly talked to his family since, and he certainly doesn't take any money from them. He goes around boycotting their products."

"Oh, don't be ridiculous," Susan said irritably. "You can't boycott C & C. They make the only J-strap mountain hinge in the world!"

Janie smirked. "Take a look in his pack sometime," she insisted. "I tell you, my sources are accurate."

Susan got up and began to clear the dishes off the table. "Your sources are pathologically addicted to sensational stories," she said stoutly. "Sometimes I wonder if you even *have* any sources. Maybe you make all this up."

"Ask Jack," Janie retorted.

Susan ran water into the sink. Of all the little pieces of information Janie had ever brought up, this had to be the most confusing. Of course it fit the pattern. Jack was stubborn and strong-willed, and Susan could easily see him breaking off a relationship over a breach of his strict code of ethics. Certainly the incident was consistent with Jack's fanatical concern for mountain safety. She had a feeling she'd just been handed a very important piece of the puzzle that was Jack Cameron, but she had no idea what to do with it.

Chagrined, she realized that she'd spent so much time fighting with the man, or kissing him, or babbling about her own problems and concerns, that she hadn't managed to learn anything about his background. She put the washed coffee cup into the drainer and decided that the time had come for her to ask him what *he* was afraid of, and what he wanted and expected, instead of spending all her time worrying about the present snag in their relationship.

The decision made her feel much lighter of heart. She could do something besides brood and worry. Maybe she'd find something in Jack's past that would help her understand him. As soon as he got back from Zürich, she'd get him alone for a nice long talk.

"Are you going to stand there daydreaming all day?" Janie asked. "You've only got forty-five minutes."

Susan wheeled sharply on her heels and stared at her assistant. "What do you mean, I've only got forty-five minutes?"

"He's due in at ten," Janie said innocently. "He called while you were in the shower."

"For Pete's sake!" Susan exclaimed. She pulled the belt of her robe more tightly around her waist and ran toward the stairs. How like Janie. She'd spend half an hour giving you a lot of useless information and forget to tell you the one important thing she knew!

Susan took the steps in a series of leaps. Jack was coming, Jack was coming. Now that that fact had sunk in, her heart was singing. She ran into her bedroom and closed the door behind her. It had been a long week. She hadn't realized until this instant just how much she'd missed him. She tore her robe off and threw it onto the bed. She *would* get Jack alone for a talk. Maybe that would help.

She hoped something would. She was beginning to realize that she wanted him too much for anything—even inevitable heartbreak—to stand in the way for long.

He didn't come at ten. He didn't come at eleven, either. By twelve Susan was tense, anxious, and a little annoyed. She stalked around the house nervously, straightening things that didn't need to be straightened and stopping to look at herself in mirrors and polished glass surfaces. The soft outlines of her pale gray cashmere sweater and flowing dirndl skirt rippled and danced as she moved, providing an attractive frame for her petite figure. Unfortunately, there was no one around to appreciate it.

At one she made herself lunch, ate half of it, and threw the rest away. She didn't really like Camembert anyway, she told herself.

At four she turned on the television and tried to watch a German situation comedy about the daily life of a bureaucrat in the post office. At four-thirty she decided there was nothing comic about it. She abandoned television for a murder mystery and lost the thread of the story every other line.

At six-thirty she served dinner to the other members of the crew, Janie Dean, and herself—and sat silently throughout the meal, poking at her potatoes with her fork. An hour later, when Jeanne St. Cloud announced that the group intended to go to bed early for once, Susan stifled a groan of relief. She couldn't possibly have taken another tour of the night life of Bresson.

"If he could call to say he was coming," Susan told Janie as they washed dishes, "then he could call to say he was held up."

Janie put the last water glass into the cupboard and said, "I think the next time the group offers to do the dishes for you, you ought to let them." She shrugged at the lethal look Susan sent her. "Well, what am I supposed to say?" she asked. "He was delayed. So he'll be here when he can get here."

"I still say he could have called," Susan stubbornly continued. "For all we know, he's sick somewhere, or dying."

"If he'd had an accident, we would have heard about it," Janie said. "There have been radios on in this house all day. He's all right, Susan. He's just been held up."

"I still say—" Susan repeated.

Janie threw the dishtowel over the edge of the sink and marched toward the door hook for her jacket. "For someone who doesn't have a case," she muttered, "you certainly have a case."

"Which is supposed to mean what?"

"I'm not even going to try to tell you." Janie jammed her arms into the jacket sleeves. "It would only start another argument. I'm going home."

"It's late," Susan said worriedly. "You shouldn't go home in the dark."

"I go home in the dark almost every day," Janie pointed out, winding a scarf around her neck. "He'll be here when he gets here," she advised. "Make yourself some hot milk and go to bed. You need your sleep." She let herself out the back door and stopped for a moment on the kitchen steps. "You know," she said thoughtfully, "I wish you could stand back and see yourself. You may think you're making sense, but your behavior is really most peculiar." Then she turned and started down the path.

Susan closed the door behind her and sighed. She probably was acting peculiarly, but she had a perfect right to. After all, no matter what Janie said, there were all kinds of accidents that weren't reported on the radio. Something really big like a train crash or a bank robbery would be, but what if something less dramatic had happened? What if Jack had become ill and confused, or been beaten up and mugged. He could be lying in some hospital somewhere, with no identification. He could be mortally wounded. He could be . . .

She was just dismissing these thoughts as ridiculous when another, equally disturbing idea occurred to her. Maybe this was how Jack felt when he saw her doing something he considered dangerous on a mountain.

She turned that notion over and over in her mind. She didn't like it. It assumed too many things. For one thing, it allowed that Jack might have a point when he exploded in an angry tirade against her—a point that left the question of her competence or incompetence completely out of the picture. Oh, she was willing to concede that Jack might sometimes be right when he told her she pulled dangerous stunts. After all, she *had* rappeled out her bedroom window that morning last week. She was glad Janie had never discovered the open window and the rope, even though she herself had had to spend most of the evening cleaning snow off her bedroom carpet.

But Jack had no way of knowing about that. He was critical and anxious even when she was behaving with perfect cautiouness. As for his feelings being like hers of this moment, well . . .

She decided to take Janie's advice and make herself a cup of hot milk. Chocolate milk, to indulge her sweet tooth. She'd bring the milk and a mystery story into the living room, stretch out on the couch, throw a down comforter over herself, and try to relax with a little light reading. She wouldn't think about the possibility that Jack's fears about some of the things she did when climbing had something in common with the way she was feeling about him. That line of thought led to too many disturbing implications.

In her dream there was a river that ended in a waterfall that cascaded over the edge of a high cliff to a valley too far below her to be seen. There was an echo, too, and lots of ropes and pitons on the mountain face.

"Dive or climb," the echo said.

"What does that mean?" the dream-Susan asked the dream-Jack who stood so far above her on the mountain face.

"Dive or climb," the dream-Jack repeated. "You've got to climb up to me or dive into the waterfall. You can't stay where you are."

"Why not?"

"Look at your feet."

Susan looked at the ground beneath her. It seemed to be cracking apart, crumbling into pebbles and sand. She shifted uneasily, looking for a solid place, a way to stay where she was. But she was standing on a small dime of earth, and there wasn't anywhere to go.

"Dive or climb," the dream-Jack's voice called down to her. "There isn't anything else you can do."

"Susan?"

Susan shifted and pulled, straining against something she thought must be air, but air that had somehow become very thick, so that moving through it was like wading in water. Then the scene dissolved, and she was left only with the sensation of something very green and cool and quiet. She was in a paradise of calm, where there was no doubt, no fear, and no loneliness.

"Susan?"

She stretched out, blinked, and stretched again. He was there, sitting next to her on the couch, his huge body propped against the sofa back. Some vestige of her waking self warned her that she should do something to protect herself, but it wasn't strong enough to make her listen. She felt too peaceful, too complete. She wanted to lie in this position forever.

"Where were you?" she asked him lazily. "You're late."

"We had a white-out at the Zürich airport. My plane couldn't take off." After a thoughtful pause, he added, "I got here as soon as I could."

"You could have called," she murmured.

"Yes," he admitted. "I probably should have."

She felt his arms slip under her and forced her eyes open.

"What are you doing?" she asked him sleepily. "I didn't want to move."

His grin was gentle, cherishing. "I'm taking you up to bed," he whispered.

"Are you really?" she whispered back, a shiver of anticipation pulsing through her. She shifted a little in his arms. It felt so good to have him holding her, so wonderful to feel his strong muscles cradling her against his chest. She huddled closer to him, wanting to feel his heartbeat.

His eyes went dark with seriousness, while his eyebrows shot up in surprise. Then that expression gave way to a new one: tender, tentative, watchful. Susan knew what he must be thinking, knew that he must find her present mood an abrupt and inexplicable change from her earlier combativeness.

It wasn't, really. The things she felt now she had felt from the first. Something—maybe the loneliness she had endured in his absence, maybe her relief at having him safely beside her again, maybe the vulnerability that accompanies the first moments of a quiet awakening—had brought those feelings to the forefront now.

And she had no desire to deny them. They had wasted so many hours fighting. Now they had a small bubble in time in which they were both completely open to each other, and she wanted to hold on to it as long as she could. She wound her arms around his neck and clung to him. His shoulders were so broad and strong. His arms were so sure of their grip. Lying against him she felt totally safe, completely at peace.

He carried her silently up the stairs and down the hall to her room. Then he lowered her, stretching her out on the snowy-white spread that covered her bed. He sat down beside her and ran a hand through her hair.

"I can't help thinking you're sleepwalking," he said huskily. "Or sleep-agreeing. Or asleep."

Susan smiled gently. "I probably am," she said with luxurious slowness. "But it doesn't matter."

"But it does." He got up and went to close the door, leaving Susan to watch the sinuous movements of his long legs. When he started back to her, she smiled, and he smiled in return. Then he sat beside her on the bed, and he was all seriousness.

"I want to make love to you," he told her in a shaking voice. "I have from the moment I first saw you. But, Susan, I don't want to reach that goal by a trick or a mistake. You're much too important to me for that. I don't want you to do anything you're going to regret tomorrow morning, or any other morning."

She put a hand up to his face. His five-o'clock shadow was curiously rough, and she found the slight abrasiveness of it against her fingers tantalizing.

"I spent the day thinking about the things I had to do before I let you get close to me," she whispered. "I'm not going to lie to you. Those things are still there. But Jack—" Her voice choked off. "I don't know," she said finally. "This last week, I've missed you so. I couldn't wait for you to get back, and when I thought of you it was the way you kissed me I remembered. And then, downstairs just now, I felt so peaceful with you beside me."

His mouth lifted in a gentle grin. "Did anyone ever tell you you don't make much sense sometimes?" he asked wryly.

"Yes, I do," Susan said urgently. "I don't know how this is going to turn out. I don't know that we're going to be able to solve the problems between us. But, Jack, when I'm not making excuses for why I shouldn't want to make love with you, then all I want is to make love with you. I want it now. For the next few hours I don't even want to think about what might happen in the future."

"I'm always thinking about it," Jack muttered, looking suddenly haggard. "It's the future that worries me." He put his hands in her hair again, this time loosening the braids that held it away from her face.

Susan liked the feeling it gave her. It was as if she had been in chains, and someone was finally setting her free.

"I know I should keep talking," Jack said helplessly.

"I know I should argue with you. But I can't."

"I couldn't either," Susan said softly. "Not now."

His hands trailed softly down the sides of her face, along her neck, to the top of her sweater. It was like a long, slow, hot tide that set everything in its path on fire. Susan felt her heart begin to pound, and she was sure the flush she felt in her face covered every inch of her.

Jack began unbuttoning her sweater, letting his fingers linger first on the fabric and then on the softness of her skin beneath. "From the first day I saw you, I've been dreaming about this," he whispered hoarsely. "I've wanted almost nothing else. Cared for almost nothing else." He drew her sweater away and looked down at the lacy bra that contained her breasts. "You were always under all that bulky clothing," he said gently, "but you could never hide what you really were. Beautiful. I always knew you were beautiful."

"I always knew you were . . . unavoidable," Susan said, laughing and sitting up a little to press herself against him. "I'm so very glad you were unavoidable."

Jack laughed, too, but it was a strangled sound. His arms moved around her back, pushing off the sweater as they went. Then his hands reached for the clasp of her bra, and Susan felt a shiver of anticipation as her rosy breasts were released to the night air and Jack's appraisal.

He bent his head, and Susan lifted her lips, ready to experience again the soaring desire his kiss always awakened in her. This time, however, the effect was much stronger. Her whole body shook with excitement and exploding desire as Jack's tongue flicked against the hollows of her mouth.

She clung to him, straining against him with more passion than she had ever thought she could feel. His hands stroked her breasts, cupping and fondling and tracing delicate circles around the pink aureoles, then teasing the sensitive nipples until they rose to rock-hard peaks. Susan fumbled wildly at the buttons of his shirt, wanting to feel the soft, downy hairs and the rippling muscles of his chest.

"Dear Lord, you're beautiful," Jack whispered desperately as his tongue darted into her ear. "Beautiful and perfect and brave. I could never get enough of you."

"I don't have enough of you yet," Susan whispered back. "Oh, please."

His hand trailed across her ribcage and stomach and tugged at the zipper of her jeans. Susan shifted on the bed, wanting to make his progress easier. A new pounding had begun, this time deep within her, and she knew even as it started that it would not be denied.

Then her jeans were stripped away, and she felt Jack's hands begin an exploration of her thighs. The insistent caresses started a flaming pulse-fire within her, and her body flared with sudden, uncontrollable explosions. Then Jack momentarily pulled away from her, and when he returned his body was free of his clothes, and his strong naked thighs pressed against her own.

"You've got hair everywhere," Susan whispered absently, reaching for him. "I want to hold and stroke and touch you everywhere."

"Leave the holding and stroking and touching to me," Jack laughed croakily. "At least for the moment."

"What's the matter?" Susan teased, letting her hand trail along the seemingly endless stretch between his knees and hips. "You have some macho thing about women being passive during lovemaking?"

"I love women who are active during lovemaking," Jask gasped. "But if you keep that up, we're not going to have much of a night."

"Oh?" She renewed her efforts. "How about that?"

Jack grasped her by the waist and ran his tongue across her navel. "Just you wait," he growled into the silky skin of her stomach. "I've got something even you can't resist."

Then he slid lower, lower, until he was pressed against that most secret part of her. His tongue flicked out, and Susan felt an inner explosion that was stronger and more compelling than anything she had ever expected could exist. The pounding of her heart was now a raging staccato of mingled fulfillment and renewed desire, and she seemed to be on fire. Then she felt something very much like an eruption of steam and flame, as if she were a volcano that couldn't hold back the fullness of its seething core a moment longer. Still his tongue probed. With each new explosion she was sure she could go no higher. With each new teasing demand of his tongue, she did. She clung desperately to him, wanting this revelation of feeling to continue forever, but needing the firmness of his body as a foundation to keep her from rocketing into space.

"I knew you'd be like this," Jack murmured as he slid up along her body, sensitizing every inch of her. "I knew you'd be the most passionate, most giving woman I'd ever known."

"I never knew it," Susan murmured as she pressed her face to his neck and gave him a soft kiss. "I never knew anything could feel like this. I never knew anyone could *make* me feel like this."

Jack half chuckled, half gasped into her ear. "That was nothing," he teased. "That was second best."

"Second best to what?" Susan asked, groggy with desire.

"Don't you feel you could go all night?" Jack tantalized her, sending a flutter of light, feathery kisses down her throat that made her spark again with passion and longing.

"All week," Susan gasped, clinging to him. "All *month.*"

Jack laughed with pleasure. "You're passionate; you're beautiful. I don't think I could care for anyone as much as I care for you—this moment and always."

Susan was about to answer him, wanted to answer him, but at that second he turned and covered her with his body. He pushed her legs open with his own and cradled his long limbs there, holding himself above her with his elbows and looking intensely into her eyes.

"So very, very beautiful," he marveled as he leaned to deposit a teasing, simple kiss on her mouth. "So very, very beautiful," he repeated as he thrust deeply into her.

Susan felt him begin to rock them, and she held his waist, matching his motion with her own. He was deep within her, and with every gliding thrust he came closer to the core of something that was much more than physical. Susan's heart began to pound again, and the resonant echoing that had begun when he touched her took on new force. He had been right. Everything was second best to this, this laser beam of total contact that made them heart and soul, bone and marrow, a part of each other. She felt as if the world had come apart and been reassembled. Nothing existed in it anymore but this fireworks display of total fullfilment, total passion, total love.

The first thing he said when they were able to talk again was "I love you."

Susan lay very still beside him on the bed, letting the breeze from the slightly open window blow across her naked, slightly sweating body. *I love you.* The words gave her a satisfaction that completed the one his body had just given her. She ran a languid finger over the soft hairs on his chest and sighed.

"I love you, too," she told him solemnly. Then she turned over to face him and smiled. "Maybe you had something there with all that talk about love at first sight."

"Love that doesn't happen at first sight doesn't happen at all," Jack murmured teasingly, though Susan was sure he meant what he said. He stroked her hair back from her temple. "I think I'm glad I didn't try to talk you out of this," he whispered.

"I am, too," Susan whispered back.

"Let's get under the covers and snuggle," he suggested.

She giggled. "If we do that," she told him, "I don't think either of us is going to get any sleep."

"No?" Jack asked innocently. He trailed his fingers along her waist, tantalizingly, enticingly.

Susan yelped and rolled away. "I've got classes in the morning," she scolded him. "Behave yourself."

"I always behave myself," he told her with mock arrogance. He dipped his tongue into the hollow at the base of her neck, making her body flame once more. "Let me show you how well I behave myself," he coaxed.

"I'm going to remember you with every ache in my body tomorrow during class," she warned him.

"Nonsense," he huffed. "This will increase your capacity for exercise nearly to infinity."

Chapter 8

WHEN SUSAN TUMBLED out of bed the next morning she was still naked, but not even the freezing draft that spilled through the partially open window could make her shiver. She looked down at Jack's nude, sleeping body, knowing that last night they'd made memories she would never be able to recall with cool objectivity. She couldn't make herself worry about the problems that had plagued their relationship from the beginning. In the rosy afterglow of last night's lovemaking, it seemed impossible that anything could ever go wrong between them again.

She was in the shower when she remembered her resolution of yesterday, and the story Janie had told her about Jack's relationship with his family. She let the pounding hot water pour through her soapy hair and considered what to do about it. She'd been too caught up in the development of her own relationship with Jack to quiz him about his life, and she was glad it had happened that way. She wouldn't have missed what had happened between them for anything in the world. Still, she wanted to know more about him, and since he never seemed to volunteer any information, she would have to ask.

She stepped out of the shower and grabbed her towel, suddenly unconcerned about the whole question. There was plenty of time to settle any questions either of them might have about the other's past. She could envision long nights of lovemaking ahead, and in their wake, long nights of talk. There would be time enough to find out everything she needed to know.

When she got back to her bedroom, Jack was awake. The quilt was draped casually around his waist, and he was sitting up in bed. Susan closed the door behind her and smiled at him.

"I'd come over and give you a kiss," she told him, "but I'd probably never make it to class."

"You're so right," Jack agreed. "Why don't you come over here anyway."

Susan wagged an admonitory finger at him and skirted the bed on her way to the closet. "I've got three sessions this morning, and the easiest is my advanced class. Janie Dean's already downstairs getting breakfast. It's time to get up and go to work."

"I'll stay here a little while longer," Jack said. "Just to watch the show."

"What show?"

He leered happily at the towel that covered her body and the bra and panties in her hand. Susan blushed, started to turn away, then realized it wouldn't do any good. He would simply get a back view instead of a front one. Feeling bolder than she ever had, Susan turned to face Jack and deliberately dropped the towel. She noted his appreciative glance with quick relief and a kind of soaring excitement. In this, Jack Cameron wasn't at all like Dan. He liked her body, and he liked her brazenness—at least when it was directed at him. Dan thought any such "display" was vulgar, even in the privacy of their bedroom.

Feeling almost as beautiful as Jack kept telling her she was, Susan dressed slowly, pulling on underwear and workout clothes with insolent seductiveness.

"The warm-up pants are going to be a letdown," she informed him cheerfully. "But duty calls."

"What do you need all that stuff for?" Jack complained. "I thought you were running simple workout sessions."

"I need the brace," Susan explained pointing to the Ace bandage that bound her left arm, "because I broke that arm skiing a few years ago. As for the rest of this stuff"—she waved a hand negligently over her layered costume, which included leotards and tights, an athletic bra, warm-up pants and sweatband—"an attack assault session is no picnic."

"Attack assault." Jack looked interested. "That's the top of the line, isn't it? The kind of thing Jeanne and Marie are doing with you?"

"That's right. But I don't work with them until the afternoon. This is my advanced class."

"Your advanced class is made up of expert climbers?"

Susan shook her head. "No. When I get expert climbers here—women training for an actual climb—they get attack assault every day for about six weeks, plus weight training, plus dance to improve their balance. My advanced class only gets attack assault once a week. It's sort of a preview of what they're in for if they get serious about climbing."

"That sounds all right," Jack mused.

Susan waited, expecting him to say something more. When he didn't, she returned to her dresser.

By the time she was ready to go downstairs, Jack had been quiet for so long she was sure he'd forgotten all about her classes. She straightened from crouching to tie the laces of her ballet practice shoes and walked over to the bed.

"I've got to go." She planted a chaste kiss on his forehead. "I'll be done around noon. I'll make you lunch."

"I'd love to have you make me lunch," Jack said, catching her in his arms and planting a kiss squarely on her lips. He held her tightly against him, grinning. "But what about now?"

"Now I'm going to work. It's Monday morning. Time to return to the wars, as you once put it."

"Different context," Jack protested. Then his gaze grew serious. "I know I'm fooling around," he said, "but what I really want to say is that I'd like to sit in on one of your classes. Would that be an invasion of privacy?"

Susan was surprised. "It's a workout," she told him. "No one's ever asked to observe before. It'd be a little boring if you're not involved in it, wouldn't it?"

"I could see what you've done with the Bernheimer," Jack suggested. "And if you've come up with something valuable for women climbers, I'd like to know about it. I climb with women a great deal."

Susan considered his proposition and finally nodded. Actually, she decided, this was a good sign. She liked the idea that he was interested in her work.

She ruffled his hair and planted another kiss on his forehead. "You get dressed," she told him. "Class starts in fifteen minutes in the dance room."

He was waiting for her when she arrived at the dance studio. She'd just finished signing checks for the bills Janie had prepared for her. He noticed her as soon as he walked in, although her students didn't. They were too busy preening and posing and trying to get him to notice them. Susan looked over her collection of girls with barely concealed amusement. Some of them were pretty—Maura Haymarket, daughter of the current chairman of the board of International Steel, might even be called beautiful—but Jack clearly wasn't interested. It occurred to Susan that there were definite advantages to a man who'd been around a little. Jack wasn't about to fall for every pretty face. He'd seen enough of them to know which one he wanted—and for the right reasons.

She grabbed the whistle she wore around her neck and blew, effectively capturing the attention of every student in the class. Even Maura Haymarket swung around sharply, ready for work—and Maura was almost never ready for work.

Susan put her hands on her hips and said, "The man in the back of the room is Jack Cameron." She ignored the excited "Oooh" that went up from the group. Since these girls came from families who vacationed every winter in climbing villages, they all knew who Jack Cameron was. Susan was not, however, willing to feed their hero-worship. "Mr. Cameron would like to observe our class," she told them dryly. "You're supposed to be the best I've got. I hope you don't prove me a liar."

The class straightened and stretched, trying to look like old mountain hands and sweet young things simultaneously. As she had hoped, her announcement about Jack had kindled the desire in each of them to do a perfect workout. The fact that they wanted to be perfect mainly in the hope that Jack would find them fascinating mattered not at all. Susan wanted them to work hard for their own sake and hers, and she didn't care why they did it.

Still, she sensed Jack knew what the girls were doing and why, and she shot him an amused wink. He grinned, and winked elaborately back.

Susan turned to her class and raised her whistle to her lips. "All right," she told them. "We're doing an attack assault sequence in thirty minutes, double-step to the count. Start with ladder climbs. When I blow, *move!*"

She pressed her whistle to her lips and gave it a long blast.

It was the best workout she could ever remember conducting. The girls behaved like veterans. Not only did they ladder climb almost faster than she did, not only did they do leg stretches that made their bodies look like they were made of rubber, but they did everything with almost inhuman speed and what was certainly inhuman posture. Susan didn't think she'd ever seen backs so straight—and they stayed straight, minute after minute, no matter how fast they worked.

Amazing what the presence of a good-looking man could do, Susan thought wryly as she put them through the last of the exercises, the run-clap sequence. This was usually twenty-five minutes long, consisting of five minutes' running in place alternating with five minutes of jumping jacks. Since they were doing the series double-time, the usual twenty-five-minute sequence took only twelve, and none of the girls missed a beat.

Susan knew that if Jack hadn't been there, her students would have been lying on the floor groaning complaints by now. They were amateurs and dilettantes, after all, not serious climbers training for an expedition. But none of them wanted to admit that they couldn't do what they thought Jack expected of them, and none of them failed her.

She brought the series to a close with a last, trailing blast on her whistle, and bent over from the waist to shake out her muscles.

"Beautiful!" she complimented her class. "Stretch out now. Relax. Sit on the mats if you want to. We're going to take five minutes."

A short, homely, but fun-loving girl named Lida Dailey let out a relieved cheer, and the rest of the class laughed. Susan laughed with them.

"Five minutes," she warned playfully. "Then I want to show Mr. Cameron the weight series."

There was a lot of good-natured grumbling but no real protest, and Susan walked to the back of the room feeling proud of them all. She was proud of herself, too. She had never felt so perfectly alive from mere exercise, or so wonderfully, beautifully in shape. It excited her to wonder what Jack might have been thinking as he watched her move. She hoped his fantasies had been as vivid as hers were now.

She dropped down onto the bench beside him and stretched, grinning. "I do that four times a day, but it never gets easy," she said. "Especially not on Monday mornings. What did you think of it?"

She turned toward him brightly, expecting to see an appreciative gleam in his eye and to hear just how impressed he was by her students' performance. Instead, she found him frowning at her, his eyes clouded. Something lurched in her stomach. They hadn't done anything wrong. She was sure of it. Why was Jack looking so—so solemn?

"Is something wrong?" she asked him. "I thought we did a perfect run."

"A perfect run at what?" he questioned. "What does this replace—if it replaces anything?"

Susan couldn't conceal her surprise. "It replaces the

Bernheimer series," she told him. "I explained all that to you the night we fixed the skylights."

If anything, Jack's expression became even darker. "You can't replace the Bernheimer series with that," he declared. "I understand about the fourth series. I could live with that. But this!" He gestured at the floor of the dance room. "You've left out nearly everything. No pull series, no back control—nothing but the run-clap. You're not going to make them ready for climbing with this. They don't have half of what they need."

Susan felt the hot flush of anger flood through her. The man had spent less than half an hour observing her class, and already he was convinced that they were second rate—that her methods were second rate! He wasn't interested in observing and understanding, only in criticizing. He wanted to make sure she toed the line—the line as he defined it.

"That's the roughest workout you'll ever see anybody do," she told him hotly. "There's enough there to strengthen anyone's back and legs and arms and feet. These girls could do a Bernheimer standing on their heads!"

"You think so?" Jack challenged. "All I've seen here so far is a lot of quasi-dance exercises—and you're using them to replace the Bernheimer! What matters on a mountain is the ability to complete a certain set of physical actions. Everything must be subordinated to that. If you don't give them that ability, you don't give them anything—no matter how good they look."

Susan began to feel a headache coming on. The energy she'd felt just a few moments before was gone, replaced by a sick rage that made her feel capable of murder.

"What's your problem, anyway?" she asked him. "Is it that you can't stand to see anyone doing anything that hasn't been given the seal of approval by a hundred years' worth of male mountain climbers, or is it me? Is it just that you don't think *I* could possibly know what I was doing?"

"You know that isn't true," Jack flared, his eyes suddenly hot with anger instead of just concern. "Don't turn this around! I'm not criticizing your abilities. I'm just saying you might have gotten carried away. You *have* been carried away once or twice. Maybe you're right that female climbers need this stuff. All I'm saying is that you should give it to them *with* the Bernheimer, not instead of it!"

Susan stood. Her body was heated and trembling, but her mind was cold and clear. Jack Cameron thought he knew everything, did he? Well, she'd show him. She'd give him a demonstration he'd never forget. And then— She forced her mind away from what would happen then. If she thought about it, she'd never be able to go through with what she was about to do.

She put her hands on her hips and looked down at him. "I take it you think that someone who'd done the series you just saw couldn't do a Bernheimer unless they'd been doing a Bernheimer all along?" she asked icily.

"Of course they couldn't," Jack insisted, though more quietly than he had a few moments before. "You must realize—"

"Never mind what I realize," Susan cut him off. "My troop has never done a Bernheimer, at least not while they've been with me. You have, however. You think you could do the series I just put them through?"

"Of course I could!" Jack exploded. "Those were just—just *grace* exercises, for heaven's sake!"

Susan gave him a tight little smile. "Hold on to your seat, Mr. Cameron. You're about to get the object lesson of your life."

* * *

It was the grimmest half hour Susan had ever spent, and she was never sure exactly how she got through it. Her students had never seen a Bernheimer, but that wasn't a problem. They were used to doing three hours of vigorous, continuous exercise at least three days a week, and Susan suspected they even looked on the new series as a welcome break in routine. As she expected, they also found it fairly easy work, even in double-time.

She hadn't devised her method from ignorance, as Jack seemed to think. She'd devised it because the Bernheimer was giving her less than what she needed. She'd started experimenting long before she reached Switzerland, and she'd been experimenting ever since. And she wasn't interested in going easy on anyone.

Every once in a while she glanced at Jack in his seat at the back of the room. When she began the series, he had looked stubborn and thoughtful. As it continued, and as it became more and more obvious that her students found the whole thing a lark, he began to look uncomfortable. By the time she reached the run-clap, he looked positively embarrassed.

Spurred on by an anger that had gone so far out of control it was nearly spite, she called triple-time on the run-clap. A few of the girls shot her furious glances, but they all fell to, and before she knew it she was flipping into a modified cheerleader's leap to announce the end of the series. She hit the ground angrier, if anything, than she had been when she first announced the Bernheimer. Physical exercise was reputed to be an outlet for rage and hostility, but this time it had been a power generator. Her fury was implacable.

"All right," she told the girls. "Take another five. It might be ten. I'll be right back."

She knew that many of them were looking at her oddly. They had sensed the tension in her, had probably even heard much of her conversation with Jack.

You wouldn't be so angry if he hadn't made love to you last night, something inside her whispered. She pushed the nagging thought away. The fact was that she was angry, and she deserved to be. Nothing else mattered.

She came to a full stop in front of Jack. "Do you think you can call that completing the Bernheimer?" she asked him coldly.

Jack hesitated. Finally he rose to his feet, his face anxious. "Susan—" he started tentatively.

Susan wasn't interested in explanations or apologies. Not now. "I asked you if you would call that successfully completing a Bernheimer," she insisted.

"Yes," Jack admitted. "It was."

"Good," she snapped. She pointed to a door behind him. "There's a changing room in there. Go get your gear, suit up, and get back here as quickly as possible. We'll be ready for you when you arrive."

"Susan, please—" Jack began.

But she wouldn't listen. "You said you could do an attack assault," she told him. "Now I want to see you do one."

Jack looked like he was about to say something else, but he didn't. He inclined his head, turned on his heel, and walked away. Susan watched him leave, her heart pounding.

She hadn't expected him to be able to do her series; she wanted to see him fail, and she wasn't disappointed. Her anger had cooled a little in the ten minutes it had taken him to find his workout clothes and get them on, but it hadn't really abated. She felt like a block of ice frozen to a temperature so low no known heat could melt her.

She knew it wasn't fair to ask him to do the exercises she had devised. A great many of his problems had nothing to do with the shape he was in, or the shape the Bernheimer method had put him into. She had devised the series to take advantage of certain natural propensities in the makeup of women's bodies.

For instance, because nature expected women to support pregnancies, the muscles in the lower back were capable of being developed further than those of men. It was one of the reasons women gymnasts could do certain displays men could not—and why she doubted that any man would ever get through the fifth sequence of her method without pain. Her method strengthened the lower back more than the upper because that was where women had their strength. For the purposes of an actual climb, it didn't really matter which was developed, as long as one or the other was.

When Jack stumbled during the hip-twists, Susan almost felt sorry for him. She'd seen some male ballet dancers do that particular move, but they'd trained for years to develop that kind of flexibility. Women had it naturally and needed only minimal exercise to keep themselves limber in the hip area. Jack had it not at all. Every time he swung his body to the right, trying to duplicate the easy sway of Maura Haymarket in front of him, Susan thought he was going to break something.

She swung into the run-clap with a feeling of relief. This, she knew, Jack would be able to do with ease. It was the way the Bernheimer method ended, too. She had decided to keep this fifth series as part of her own program because she didn't trust her students to get the running she knew they needed if they were ever going to climb a mountain. Students, especially beginners, tended to think their responsibilities were over as soon as teacher wasn't looking.

She wound the series down, letting her feet move more and more slowly as the seventy-five double-beat taps came to an end. Jack looked tired and strained, but she tried not to pay any more attention to him. She must have made her point, and she didn't want to get into another shouting match with him now that it was over. She was tired herself, and more than physically. She just wanted to get him out of her dance room so she could get on with her classes.

She stopped running, bent over at the waist, and touched her toes. Then she straightened up again and looked over her class, carefully avoiding Jack's eyes. Her students were beginning to look a little weary, and she didn't blame them.

"You were wonderful," she told them, wishing she could force more emotion past the ice in her throat. "I think we'd all agree we've had enough for one day. I don't think I could do any more without collapsing myself."

"Hear, hear," Lida Dailey cheered weakly, and the rest of them laughed.

Even Susan managed a smile, though she doubted it was very convincing. "Go steam up the showers," she told them. "I'll see you all here tomorrow at nine. Maybe we can talk about scheduling a training climb sometime soon."

Most of the tired faces instantly looked brighter, and Susan promised herself that she wouldn't forget to plan that training climb. The girls in this class were itching to get out on a real mountain, and after this morning she was inclined to think they'd earned it. She watched them trail across the studio floor to the shower room.

She turned to Jack only when the room was empty and there was nothing left to do but get on with it. He was standing with his feet wide apart, doing a series of jerks and pulls, the classic method for relieving cramped leg and shoulder muscles. Every once in a while he winced, and Susan knew his back was aching.

"Do a complete back bend," she told him wearily. "Hold it as long as you can. Keep doing them until it feels like it's straightened out. It shouldn't take long."

She knew he was about to say something, but she wasn't ready to hear him. She turned away and hurried out of the dance room. In the shape he was in, he'd never be able to catch up with her.

She managed to avoid Jack—and everyone else—for the rest of the day. She knew he was lurking outside the door while she conducted her classes, and once he even came in, but she ignored him and he didn't interrupt her. When her last class was over she ducked into a passageway at the back and hurried outside by a door he wasn't familiar with.

She had dinner in Bresson—one croissant, three cups of coffee, and a piece of chocolate torte. Everything but the torte she had to force down, and she couldn't help being amused that even a devastating day like this one couldn't dampen her fondness for chocolate. It was the first glimmer of humor she'd had since she wound up the first attack assault series, and she savored it. Maybe the world wasn't going to end after all, she decided. Maybe she'd even be able to go home and get some sleep.

She waited until well after ten, strolling aimlessly through the streets of the tiny village. She stopped for a long time in front of a shop window full of tiny alpine dolls in authentic antique costumes, then again in front of a window displaying antique musical instruments. Nothing really registered. She was too tired to think.

When she finally started home she was nearly asleep

on her feet. Only her reluctance to face what was waiting for her made her walk instead of splurge on a taxi. She even considered trying to climb *up* the side of the chalet to her bedroom window, but although the idea was tempting, she finally rejected it. She didn't have her gear, and even if she did, she had no way to climb a sheer face she couldn't drive a piton into. If she tried to put a steel pin into the side of her chalet she'd either electrocute herself or bring the house down.

She paused one last time at her front door, did her now customary counting-to-ten routine, and told herself that confrontation was good for the soul. Then she let herself in.

He was waiting for her in the living room, one lamp on. He rose and came to meet her as soon as she entered. He stopped before he came too close, his expression tentative, his movements oddly ungainly.

She closed the door behind her and said nothing. After a few moments of silence he cleared his throat loudly and shifted his feet.

"Are you still speaking to me?" His voice was even, but his eyes were pleading and watchful, as if he expected another angry outburst.

Susan sighed and sat down on the stairs.

"I'm still speaking to you," she told him, cupping her chin in her hands. "But I'm very tired, and I don't want to talk this out right now. I just want to sleep."

He came to sit beside her. "Will you at least let me apologize?" he asked. "I know I behaved like a complete idiot this morning, and I'm sorry for it. I even have an explanation of sorts."

"Do you?" Susan asked, unconvinced.

Jack put his hands on his knees and seemed to collect his thoughts. "Susan, it's not an easy thing, you know, leading an expedition. It's even harder for someone like me. There are seven members of this crew besides me. I'm responsible for the lives of every one of them. I take that responsibility very seriously."

"And you think I don't take my responsibilities seriously?" she snapped, the last remnants of this morning's anger bursting through her weariness. "You've decided I'm the sort of person who plays dice with the lives of people who depend on me?"

"Not at all," Jack protested. He gave a small sigh of frustration. "All I'm trying to tell you is that there's a lot of pressure on me, leading an expedition, especially one this dangerous. I get very worried, very tense. I start thinking of all the things that could go wrong, and my blood runs cold. I—" For a moment his gaze seemed very far away, and then he snapped into the present. "I behaved like a complete fool, and there's no excuse for that. I can apologize, but that's all I can do. I wanted, however, to offer an explanation. I didn't blow up that way because I doubted your abilities or your character. I was just reacting to the pressures inside myself."

Curious, Susan looked at him. What had caused that faraway look in his eyes just then? And what should she think of his explanation?

She longed to tell him that the problem wasn't his cautiousness but his lack of trust, because as far as she could tell he trusted her neither as a professional nor as a person. She bit back the words. They would only start another long discussion, she knew, and she didn't have the heart for it. Besides, he was apologizing. Maybe that was enough for now.

She felt his hand on her arm and looked down at the fingers trailing along the sleeve of her jacket. Both arm and hand seemed to belong to people she didn't know. Their raptures of the night before felt an eternity away.

She stood up slowly, brushing away his touch. "I've got to go to sleep," she told him.

He reached for her again, this time to take her hand. "You don't have to sleep alone," he said gently. "Last night wasn't the only way it can be. It can also be restful and healing."

Some small part of her wanted to say yes, but she suppressed it. She drew away from him and said, "I do have to sleep alone. I have to think."

"Are you really going to get any thinking done tonight?" he asked wryly.

Susan shrugged. She knew no answer she could give would make any difference, so she just turned around and walked slowly up the stairs.

The short walk to her bedroom felt like a trek of a million miles.

Chapter 9

SUSAN HAD EXPECTED her depression to vanish with sleep, but it didn't. She arose in the cold, predawn darkness feeling leaden and anxious, as if something very important in her life had been cut away from her. But that was silly, she told herself. Jack hadn't been "cut away" from her. He had apologized. Nothing had ended.

But the feeling that worse was to come persisted, and Susan found herself dragging out the process of dressing. She thought of the morning before and became more depressed still. It was odd how the same action could have entirely different meanings when performed under different conditions. Odd and annoying in ways she couldn't quite define. If only she could come to some conclusion about what she felt and what she wanted to do about what she felt. Things happened between Jack and her, and she had no way to judge them.

She knew what she wanted to feel. She wanted to believe that their fight in the dance room had been mostly her fault, that she had lost her temper before she had a reason to. After all, she told herself over and over again, she was the one who had started shouting. Jack had made a simple objection. She could have answered him in a dozen ways other than the one she'd chosen.

It wasn't going to work. Wishing didn't make things so, and the fact was that she'd had a perfectly good reason to be furious with the man. He'd attacked her without knowing all the facts. He'd assumed that whatever she was doing was wrong—as far as she could tell, because it was she who was doing it. Every time she thought about his sarcastic comments on the method it had taken her so long to devise, she was ready to explode all over again.

His angry words weren't all she remembered. Their night of lovemaking hung in her memory like a Technicolor instant replay, and nothing would banish it. Even in retrospect his touch had the power to make her shiver. If she closed her eyes, she could actually feel his lips parting hers, and a shower of meteoric sensations coursed through her, leaving her knees weak. She realized disgustedly that if she could find a way to compromise her principles, she would—and all for the sake of a man who spent most of his time making her impossibly furious.

As she buckled her safety belt, ran out of her room, and headed for the kitchen and her parka, she told herself that for the rest of that day she was going to stop acting like a damn fool. She was going to act like the perfect professional, and if Jack Cameron wanted to interfere with that, he could just try.

This new, belligerent attitude made her agitated rather than happy, but it was a kind of support, and she clung to it. The crew was assembling at the base of the east face this morning to make their first group training climb, and she knew she was going to need all the strength she could find. Jack would be bound to want to practice some fancy maneuvers.

Under other circumstances—with a different expedition leader, for instance—she might have mentioned that she was dead tired and a little worried about making mistakes on the face. But today she had no intention of letting fatigue get in the way of showing that man that she was just as competent—if not more so—than he was. With any luck, he wouldn't notice she was late.

She needn't have worried. Even before she reached the end of the path that led to the clearing at the base of the east face, she could hear the sound of laughter interspersed with shouted numbers that meant the crew was still doing an equipment check. It was a general equipment check, too, Susan realized. They were calling numbers from a group stock, not verifying the equipment each climber was carrying. Either everyone had been late this morning, or Jack intended to haul a lot of metal up a simple thousand-foot face.

She slipped into the clearing and joined a group consisting of Jeanne St. Cloud, Marie Marten, and Otto Freer. They seemed to be standing around doing nothing, and they didn't look happy about it.

"What's going on?" she asked. "Where's Jack?"

Marie Marten tossed her blond curls, a gesture that held a depth of annoyance only a Frenchwoman could give it. "He is counting his equipment," she said bitingly. "All morning, he has been counting his equipment. He thinks we are going up Everest on our hands and knees!"

"He is a maniac," Jeanne agreed. "Look at this face. It is for children."

Susan didn't think the ascent was exactly for children, but Jeanne was a master climber, and she was entitled to her opinion. Susan looked curiously in the direction of the equipment pile Jack had established at the base. He was standing over it, counting something.

Susan supposed they were pitons. Theoretically, each piton was removed as the last member of the crew in line passed it, which meant that a climbing party needed a total of crew number plus one to make an ascent. In practice, things rarely worked out so neatly. Pitons were lost or broken, and some were left in the mountain face when it was determined it would be too dangerous to remove them. Any expedition leader worth the name was overly cautious about pitons. It was much better to bring too many than too few.

Jack had taken that maxim to its logical conclusion. Or absurd conclusion, she thought, eyeing what appeared to be a mini-mountain of metal. He had enough pitons piled up to scale the Matterhorn with a ten-person line.

"You see what we mean?" Marie said. "He is a crazy person. It is an astonishment that he has not brought air tanks."

"What will he do when we've got to climb?" Otto asked anxiously. "We'll be too loaded down with equipment to move!"

"We'll be too loaded down with equipment to move today!" Marie retorted. "He wishes to turn us into pack animals, that's what."

Susan took another look at the pile. It was not all pitons, she realized. There were safety ropes and webbing and hinges and T-hooks and swing holds. Good Lord! What did Jack think he was doing?

Something told her that if she wanted to keep the promises she had made to herself this morning, her best bet would be to stay as far away from Jack as possible. Even looking at him from a distance made her nervous and tense, half spoiling for a fight and half ready to throw herself into his arms. Besides, she was sure that if she even hinted she was willing to talk to him, he'd plunge into a discussion of what had happened between them yesterday, and she didn't want that. Her ragged night had left her much too close to coming unglued.

Even so, she couldn't stop herself from wandering closer and closer to that equipment pile. The nearer she came, the more fascinating it became. Aside from the items she had already noticed, she made out two steel-web etriers and a slide basket, and she was almost sure she saw a piton gun. But piton guns were almost never used, even on the most difficult ascents. Marie Marten was right. Jack was insane!

She was almost standing beside him before he noticed her, and even then he seemed to stare at her a few seconds before recognition dawned. His preoccupation annoyed Susan even more. She'd spent the whole night agonizing about their relationship, and here he was, practically announcing that he'd had his mind on more important matters. Had their fight—and their night together—affected him so little that he could completely forget it in the press of preparations for a training climb?

A moment later Susan knew he hadn't been completely unaffected. If he had been tense while she watched him from the safe distance of Marie's group, he was twice as tense now. His eyes bored into hers with a steely look that could have been either hostility or wariness, and his hands, which had been nervously ruffling his hair while he counted, were now clenched into fists. Susan felt her own tension rise, and with it the residue of yesterday's anger and this morning's black mood. It wouldn't take much to set them off again. But why? Last night he had seemed so conciliatory.

Last night he had also said he was very tense leading a climb, she remembered. But this wasn't really a climb. It was just a training ascent.

She was standing stock still, debating what to do, when Jack moved. He backed away from her, moving very slowly until he reached the mountain face and was able to lean against it.

"If you came to talk about yesterday," he said in an even voice that did nothing to hide his strain, "I can't do that now. I have to concentrate on the ascent."

Susan flushed hotly. She *had* been thinking of saying something about their fight, but she wasn't going to let him know that now. If he could be coolly professional no matter what was happening between them, then so could she. If anything, she should be cooler than he. He was the one who was always professing to be in love.

"I came to ask you about all this," she said icily, gesturing toward the equipment. "Do you really expect us to drag it up that face?"

Jack's eyes darkened. "We may need it," he bit out. "I was thinking we should all carry two safety ropes. That way, if we have to make webs, we won't run out of rope."

Susan was so startled she almost forgot to be angry. *"Make* webs?" she repeated incredulously. "But, Jack, you've got enough prefab webs to cross the polar icecap! There aren't any crevasses on that face. It's just a rock cliff!"

"You never know," Jack said ominously. "The principle of the thing is to be prepared for anything. What if we got to that ledge"—he pointed to an outcrop about a thousand feet up—"and found out it was split? What would we do then?"

"Jack," Susan said patiently, "I've been on that ledge. It's not split. It's a solid rock plateau, even bigger than the one we met on. We could camp out there for weeks on end."

"You never know," Jack repeated stubbornly. "What if there were an avalanche?"

"An *avalanche?*" Susan exclaimed. She couldn't believe what she was hearing. The man must have hit himself on the head and developed some sort of mental aberration. "For Pete's sake," she told him, "it hasn't been above freezing in this part of the Alps for two months. You need a thaw to make an avalanche!"

Jack folded his arms across his chest with an air of finality. "It is customary for crew members to accept the decisions of their expedition leader without question. It's necessary for the safety of the climb. I say we need to get this equipment up that face, and we're going to get it there."

"Not without making your entire crew mutiny," Susan snapped, stung by the hostile, impersonal way he was quoting chapter and verse of the mountain guide at her. "Your own books say it's just as dangerous to overload a crew as to underload it. You've got enough junk in that pile to build your own NASA central!"

"If the crew wants to talk to me, they can talk to me," Jack said, turning his back to her. "I'll tell them the same thing I told you. In my judgment, this is what we need on this climb, and this is what we're going to take."

"Eight pounds," Marie Marten said when they finally reached the outcrop. "I have lost eight pounds. There is no question about it."

"You can eat Sachertorte for dinner," Jeanne said. "It might do your disposition some good."

"There is nothing wrong with my disposition that the curing of that crazy man wouldn't alleviate," Marie said. "But I fear that is not to be expected."

Susan chucked her day pack onto the ground and sat

on it. It had been a long, hard climb up, worsened by the fact that she was carrying six pitons, three hinges, two safety ropes, and half a dozen tight coils of webbing. Jack had spoken to her exactly twice, once to say he wanted her rappel rope tied on with a hitch knot instead of a slip, and once to inform her that she was to take every inch of the face at a tack. In fact, they'd all taken every inch of the face at a tack. It had taken them nearly four hours to make what should have been a two-hour climb.

Jeanne and Marie were still muttering, and Susan felt all her sympathy go out to them. Jack had been putting them through hell, and as far as Susan could tell, he didn't care. He obviously intended to keep that stubborn look on his face for the duration.

Susan sat up, took the pack out from behind her, and began to unload it. The least she could do for herself was have lunch. Maybe a little food would improve *her* disposition.

She was just coming to the conclusion that Jack's studied indifference to her this morning might have its good points—it did, after all, keep them from fighting—when she felt rather than saw a shadow fall across her. Even before she looked up she knew who was there.

Trying to stay calm, she swiveled slowly and straightened up. He was standing only a few feet away from her, shoulders hunched, face white, waiting. Susan had a sudden irrational desire to do something to appease him. But last night he had been the one who'd found it necessary to apologize. She had no idea what had prompted his attitude toward her this morning.

She shoved her hands into her pockets and gazed up— way up—at him. "Well," she said lamely, feeling more ill at ease than she had the night he'd picked her up for dinner, "did you want to talk to me?"

Jack nodded but said nothing. Susan felt the first sting of annoyance at his silence. The man could certainly talk well enough when he wanted to. Evidently he didn't want to now.

"What did you want to talk to me about?" Susan offered, trying not to sound as exasperated as she felt.

"Weight contrast," Jack said abruptly.

Susan was startled. She'd heard about weight contrasting, a system that alternated heavier crew members with lighter ones on the climbing line, but she'd never tried it. The usual composition of a line was heaviest first, lightest last, based on the assumption that the heaviest members of a crew would be strong enough to hold anyone who might slip below them. Susan found weight contrasting an intriguing idea, especially since a mixed crew practicing weight contrast always had some women at the front, or "exploratory," end of the line. She was all for that. Under most circumstances she would have jumped at the chance to get some firsthand experience of the method.

This, however, was not most circumstances. Right now she wanted to convince Jack to use a traditional line.

"If we use weight contrast," Susan ventured, "would that mean you lead and I partner?"

Jack nodded. "That's exactly what it means," he agreed, his eyes hard. "First me, then you, then Otto, then Jeanne, and on down. That would be optimum."

Susan bit her lip. Jack hadn't brought up the most important consideration—that, based on the little evidence they had, they didn't climb together well. That they were also fighting made it worse. Personal animosities between crew members were bad enough. Between partners, hostility could be catastrophic. If Jack was as intent on ensuring the safety of his crew as he said he was, he should want to keep them as far apart as possible.

Susan cast around for a diplomatic way of saying what she knew she had to, came up with nothing, and decided to plunge right in. "We've been snapping at each other all day," she said slowly. "If we partner up on the descent, we're just going to get on each other's nerves." The phrase she wanted to use was much stronger than *get on each other's nerves,* but she doubted it would do much to relieve the tension between them.

Jack's face was stiff with stubbornness. "This is a climb," he told her. "On a climb I leave my emotions at the base. If you're a professional, then I expect you do, too."

"It has nothing to do with being a professional!" Susan protested. "Jack, look at the way we're behaving right this minute. We're so tense we're electrifying the air!"

"I'm behaving in a perfectly objective, professional manner," Jack insisted in a flat voice. "I don't know about you."

Susan felt as if her head would burst with anger. Of all the manipulative, arrogant, insulting attitudes! The man never missed a trick. Get him out on a mountain and he reverted to true form every time. She had half a mind to haul off and slug him one just to get it out of her system.

She clenched her fists, tightened the muscles in her arms, and tensed every other muscle in her body. Then she made a conscious effort to relax each muscle in turn. It was an effective way to calm one's anger and she certainly needed to be calm now. Jack was obviously intent on descending with a weight-contrast line. If she tried to offer any real opposition, he would fight tooth and nail to see that his choice prevailed. Then the line would be endangered no matter who won the argument, because the hostility between them would affect every other member of the crew.

She was just going to have to grin and bear it, she decided. If Jack wanted weight contrast, he'd get it without another peep out of her. They had a thousand feet of sheer rock face to get down before they reached the safety of the base, and Susan intended to finish that project in one piece. *Then* she'd let him know what she thought of this idiocy.

"All right," she told him. "We partner up. When do we start?"

"Right now," Jack said hurriedly, already turning to walk toward the boulder where he'd left his day pack.

"Right now?" Susan called after him in protest. "But Jack, we just got here. No one's had a chance to sit down yet, never mind have lunch."

"We're running late," Jack said, still stubborn. "I don't want to be climbing after dark."

Susan was ready to point out that they had six more hours before dark, but she didn't. It would only start another argument. Instead, she started shouldering her day pack and running through a routine equipment check. There didn't seem to be anything else to do.

The other members of the crew were not as cooperative.

"If he wants to go now," Marie Marten said, "he can go by himself. I'm eating cheese."

"If he keeps this up, I will quit the climb," Jeanne said. "I will do the Maidenhorn by myself."

Otto just sighed. "I would do the Maidenhorn myself, but I don't have the money. Also, not the brains to think of a plan for the east face." He grinned at them all. "He is getting worse and worse, but he's still the best there is. If he says go, I suppose I go. Even if I am very tired."

The rest of them apparently agreed with him—at least about Jack's money, brains, and abilities as an expedition leader—because they began to suit up. Susan slipped into the line beside Jack and concentrated on tying the link rope hitched to his belt onto hers. Remembering his criticisms on the ascent, she made a double hitch knot and pulled to ensure it was secure.

He took the knot out of her hand, tugged the rope himself, then leaned over to get a better look at her handiwork.

"Do it again," he told her brusquely. "It's giving a quarter inch."

"A quarter inch?" Susan echoed. "Most hitch knots give twice that. This is tight as a drum."

"Do it again," Jack insisted.

Susan yanked the knot apart and retied it with swift, short, furious tugs. If things were starting this way, the rest of the climb was going to be a doozy. She snapped the knot into place and held it up for his inspection. "How's that?"

It didn't soothe her anger when he took another long moment to inspect her work. When he nodded, indicating satisfaction, she was more inclined to kick him for his smug, superior air than thank him for the compliment. She did neither. She just watched him go over the edge, waited until he called to her, then went over the edge herself.

The breeze that blew through her hair as she slipped onto the face felt like the breath of freedom, and she reveled in it. This was a harder climb than the training ascents she set up for her students, and even the bad blood between her and Jack couldn't spoil the exhila-

ration she felt from using her abilities to the full after so
long a hiatus. She made hop jumps from the first two
pitons, then swung into a tack. It was too bad Jack
wouldn't let them hop jump all the way down. This face
was made for that maneuver, and it would be exciting
to careen down it like a tennis ball bounced against a
wall.

She was a little more than halfway down when she
realized that Jack had stopped, hooked his feet into etriers,
and appeared to be resting. She stopped, too, her hand
going automatically to her belt for the webbing to build
herself a swing. Then she saw him shake his head and
motion to her to come to him.

That was odd. Usually when Jack wanted to talk to
one of them, he tacked backward and met them on their
own ground.

She pulled the line to let Otto, who was behind her,
know she was going to need more rope. Then she swung
into a back tack and started to make her way to Jack's
piton.

"What is it?" she asked as she hitched her etrier webbing over his and shoved her feet into the slings. "I don't
like doubling up like this. I'm never sure the pins are
going to hold."

"I placed the pins myself," Jack said, dismissing her
concern. "I wanted to talk to you about your tacking."

"What's wrong with my tacking?" Susan exploded.
"I'm making it down nearly as fast as you are, and that
isn't easy when you're more than a foot taller than I am."

"You're doing a twist tack," Jack said patiently. "I
want you to do a straight tack. Twists aren't safe on a
sheer face."

Susan stared at him. She wanted to tell him where to
get off, but she couldn't do that while they were five

hundred feet in the air. Unfortunately, she couldn't do a straight tack, either. She started rocking back and forth in the etriers, counting to ten.

"I can't do a straight tack," she said finally, glad to hear how calm she sounded.

Jack was anything but calm. "You mean you don't know how?" he asked in alarm.

"Of course I know how," Susan exclaimed in annoyance. "But I haven't done one in years. I'm five feet three, for heaven's sake. It isn't feasible."

"Why would being five feet three make straight tacking unfeasible?" Jack bit sarcastically on every word.

"Because it takes too long." Susan tried to be patient. "I'd hold up the entire line. We wouldn't be able to maintain an even speed. Besides, this is the first time I've ever heard anyone say twist tacking was dangerous on a sheer face."

Jack's face grew thunderous. "I've done a lot of climbing," he told her, "and I say twist tacking is dangerous on a sheer face. The priority here isn't speed. It's finding the best way down a face without causing an accident. I want you to straight tack the rest of the way down."

"Maybe I'll rappel," Susan exploded at him. "That would really give you something to worry about."

Jack gave her a long, angry look. "Straight tack the rest of the way down," he repeated ominously. Then he hooked himself out of his etriers and began to let out his rope for the tack to the next piton.

Susan watched him go with a mixture of anger and helplessness. She accepted the fact that she sometimes pulled dangerous stunts. It had taken Jack to make her realize it, but she was ready to admit it now. But this was completely ridiculous. There wasn't a mountaineering book in the world that said anything about the relative safety of straight versus twist tacks. A climber used one method or the other purely from personal preference. Jack wasn't just being overcautious now; he was being stupid.

Susan had to stifle the rebellious thought that, faced with actually having to climb with her, Jack was behaving as Dan had, undercutting her confidence. It was true that his criticisms today had been arbitrary, and that they had been delivered in a manner almost designed to ignite her anger, but she told herself there could be lots of reasons for that.

The worst possible reason was that she had been right all along. Maybe Jack didn't respect her competence as a climber. Maybe he only wanted her on the Maidenhorn ascent because he needed women and because he thought her inadequacies could be rendered harmless if he just rode herd on her enough.

She hit the ground with aches in her back and thighs that threatened to topple her. Once started on a straight tack, she had been unwilling to hold up Otto and the rest of the crew, and she had pushed herself harder than she should have to make up the speed. It took a lot of concentration, and that at least got her mind off Jack, which was just as well. If she'd been thinking about Jack as she came down that face, she probably would have killed them all. Deliberately.

She shrugged her day pack off her shoulders and dumped it onto the ground. She was still angry, but she was still hungry, too, and right now hunger seemed to take priority. Besides, if she tried to confront Jack in the mood she was in, she would only explode again. Her suspicions about his assessment of her abilities had been growing throughout the last half of the climb. Jack could say whatever he wanted, but if the way he'd been behaving wasn't a subtle way of telling her he thought she was half-idiot and half-ox, she'd eat her cap.

She was extracting cheese from a plastic bag in her pack when she once again felt him behind her. This time she decided to ignore him. Concentrate on Brie, she told herself.

He came closer, too close to ignore. "I just wanted to ask..." he began.

Susan looked up, wondering what he could possibly have left to say to her after this disastrous climb. She caught him just as his expression began to turn from thoughtful to worried.

"Why is everything in those plastic bags?" he asked.

"To keep it sanitary," Susan said. "Why do you think?"

"Doesn't it take up a lot of space?"

She shrugged. "I've never thought about it."

"But you have to think about it," he said. "When we go up the face, you're going to have to get as much in your pack as it can possibly take. We're going to be climbing for two weeks."

Susan couldn't believe the man. "Now you're criticizing the way I package my food? For Pete's sake, I could get enough stuff in my pack to last a month!"

"Not if you wrap everything up in those plastic bags," he insisted. "I've never thought about packs before. Maybe I'll inspect all of them before we leave."

Susan felt something very much like a gunshot go off in her head. She'd been this angry before only once or twice in her life, and she knew she should go off to cool down before she even considered talking to Jack.

She didn't care. It had been a long day, and she'd had just about enough of Mr. John Randolph Cameron.

"I've spent this entire day listening to your picky, stupid, insulting criticisms," she told him, "and I've had about all I can take. All I'm ever going to take. You don't like the way I tie my ropes, you don't like the way

I pack my day pack, you don't like the way I tack—are you sure there isn't anything else? Would you like to inspect my shoelaces?"

"I've been saying the same things to everyone else," Jack flared. "That's my job. I have to concern myself with the behavior of my crew. Their safety depends on it."

"If you had any sense, you'd concern yourself with your own behavior," Susan retorted. "I've been listening to a lot of words from you, Jack, but what it comes down to is this: You don't trust me. You never have. You never will."

"Trust has nothing to do with it!" Jack exclaimed.

"Trust has everything to do with it," Susan insisted. "There are all kinds of trust in the world, Jack. You don't trust me to behave like a reasonably intelligent adult human being. I don't know why that is, but I don't care anymore. All I'm sure of is this: You may say you love me—for a while there you were very fond of *insisting* you loved me—but it's a sham. A man doesn't fall in love with someone he thinks is an incompetent fool, which is how you think of me."

"I can't say boo to you without your deciding I'm treating you like an incompetent fool!" Jack said furiously. "You don't know the difference between honest criticism and an insult, and apparently you have no interest in learning. You've got a chip on your shoulder so big you've lost all perspective on what constitutes acceptable mountain practice and what's sheer stupidity—and clearly you think it's a condition of any personal relationship that the difference not be explained to you. Well, listen to this." He stepped closer, reaching out to grab her by the shoulders and shake her. "I do love you, Susan Reed. But I'm a mountain climber as well as a lover, and I'm in charge of this crew. As long as you're on it, you're going to take criticism, follow orders, and stick to the rules."

Even in her anger, Susan could feel the flame of sensuality Jack's touch always aroused in her, but now its heat was absorbed by her white-hot anger. She grabbed his wrists and shoved him away, her whole body trembling with fury.

"Fine," she told him. "Then I'm no longer a member of this crew. And as for whatever else I once thought was going on between us—I don't have words that begin to describe how I feel about that right now. Get out of my life, Mr. Cameron. Get out of my house, get out of my dreams, get out of my way."

Blind and weak with rage, she snatched her pack from the ground and spun around toward the path.

Chapter 10

SHE DIDN'T SEE Jack again for three days. After the fight she took a long walk in the mountains, and when she returned to the chalet his things were gone. Even the tie he'd been wearing when he returned from Zürich, which had lain folded on her dresser after their night of love-making, had disappeared.

Susan tried to tell herself it didn't matter, that it was just as well he was gone. She was a fool to have gotten involved with him in the first place. She'd be much better off without him.

It didn't help. She was even more depressed than she'd been after their fight about her classes. She kept starting awake in the middle of the night, having dreamed of feeling his strong arms wrapped around her, of feeling the hot, sweet touch of his kiss. Every time someone came up behind her, her skin tingled with anticipation. Her disappointment when she turned and found only Janie Dean, or Marie Marten, or Otto, or anyone else, was swift and devastating. Somehow, when he was out of her sight, she could only remember the good things about their time together.

It might have been easier if she'd been able to talk about it, but she soon found that Jack had disappeared from her chalet in more ways than one. No one ever mentioned his name. Susan assumed he was meeting the remaining members of the crew for training climbs in the mornings, but although they talked often about their time on the mountain, they never said anything about Jack. Even Janie seemed to have acquired a case of amnesia on the subject. Whenever Susan brought up his name, Janie changed the subject.

By Friday Susan felt as if she'd been run over by a truck that had backed over her again just to make sure it finished the job. She walked out of her last class ready to take a long shower and get to sleep before dinner. She was so tired she wasn't even hungry.

Janie caught up to her in the hall outside her bedroom. Susan looked at the thunderously determined face of her assistant and had to stifle a desire to run in and lock the door. What was on Janie's mind now?

"Claire Holloway," Janie announced as soon as she reached the door.

Susan groaned. "Not tonight," she pleaded. "The last thing I want is to spend a couple of hours listening to a lot of drunken idiots blather about things they know nothing about."

"A lot of *rich,* drunken idiots," Janie persisted. She looked decidedly unsympathetic. "You skipped last week," she pointed out. "And you skipped the week before that. There are other climbing schools in the Alps, you know. And their owners go to Claire's parties."

"Maybe their owners are also drunken idiots," Susan complained. "Janie, please. I've got a headache, and I'm dead tired. I'd make a terrible impression even if I did go."

"I'd go for you if I could," Janie admitted grudgingly,

"but I wasn't invited, and you know Claire hates dealing with peons. So does the rest of that crowd. They expect the real VIP and no substitutions. Besides, if you didn't go, it would look..." Janie hesitated. "Funny," she pronounced finally.

Susan peered at her curiously. Janie looked more embarrassed than Susan had ever seen her. She was staring at the floor and the ceiling and the walls—anywhere but into Susan's eyes.

"Funny? How?" Susan asked her cautiously.

Janie managed to stare directly at the top button of Susan's shirt. "Funny," she repeated. "You know, after everything that's been going on up here. I mean, it's all over the village, and people might think..."

"That's okay," Susan said quickly. "I know what people might think." They'd think Jack had been in the right in their argument, and that she was too ashamed to face him. She knew she didn't dare leave the people who attended Claire's parties with that impression. Her fight with Jack had been about safety, and she was asking these people to trust their daughters to her care. She couldn't let them think she was admitting to being a careless, reckless incompetent. Her business would never survive.

"I hate the idea of going up there tonight," she complained to Janie. "All those people, all that noise—"

"It would look funny," Janie reiterated.

Susan nodded in reluctant agreement. "I know it would," she said ruefully. "I suppose I'll go. That's one more thing I have to hold against Jack."

Janie behaved as if she hadn't heard a word of Susan's last sentence. "Take a nap," she said, hurrying away. "I'll wake you in time to shower and dress."

Susan watched her pert blond assistant until she disappeared at the head of the stairs. Lying down on her bed, she felt ready to do anything to get out of this stupidity. Not that a night alone at home was such an inviting prospect. She'd probably spend the time moping, or, worse, dreaming about Jack. She'd had enough of that for a lifetime. But Claire Holloway's!

Susan could just picture the scene. The great, high-ceilinged reception room with its made-to-order fake antique rafters; the long table covered with a white linen tablecloth and anchored at each end by boat-sized crystal punchbowls full of something green and lethally alcoholic; the jet-setters in their one-of-a-kind evening dresses that each cost enough to run Susan's school for half a year; the climbers in their gear, appointed jesters at the feast; Jack.

Jack!

She sat up abruptly on the bed, jerked erect by the surge of adrenaline that coursed through her at her realization. Of course. She should have thought of it before. *Everybody* went to Claire's parties, and if everybody went, then . . .

She made herself lie back down, did her tense-and-relax routine, and tried to think. She'd stay away from him. She wouldn't even talk to him. After all, she had no reason to talk to him now. It shouldn't matter to her at all that he would be there.

But it did. Oh, it certainly did. She felt so dizzy she had to close her eyes against the whirling of the room. The thought of being close to him, of hearing his voice, of feeling his arm against her own, even in a casual, unintentional brush, melted her muscles and bones and nerves into a pool of hot liquid.

She had only worn the dress once before. It was not her usual kind of thing. Its ice-blue satin folds covered her arms and dropped with uncluttered elegance to the floor, but they left much of her shoulders and a great deal of her breasts bare. She'd taken it out of the closet just to try it on, but once she'd seen herself in the mirror she couldn't give it up. That will show him, some irrational part of her said. She'd attract every other man in the room.

Why it was so important that Jack see her attracting every other man in the room, she didn't know and didn't want to know. She was too intent on keeping up an appearance of calm. When Claire Holloway bustled out of her reception room to throw overeager arms around Susan, Susan had to will herself not to look over the woman's shoulder to see who was at the party.

"We haven't seen you in so long!" Claire trilled, hugging Susan to her side as she guided them both into the big room. "We thought you'd become a hermit."

"No, no," Susan apologized as best she could. "I've just had a lot of work to do." Claire was a big woman with too many teeth and breath like last night's whiskey, but her patronage was too important to the school for Susan to dare alienating her. "I would have come if I could," she told the older woman.

"We know you've been busy." Claire wagged her finger in Susan's face. "We've all heard about that. You're just going to have to tell me your side of it."

Susan grimaced in spite of herself. She was hardly likely to confide in Claire Holloway. "There really aren't any sides," she said hastily. "Mr. Cameron and I have climbing styles that are completely incompatible, that's all. I thought it would be better for the expedition if I bowed out."

Claire made an elaborate face that said she just *knew* that wasn't the whole story. "These lovers' tiffs," she sighed. "When I was your age—"

Susan finally managed to break the woman's hold, and just in time. Good grief. That was all she needed: Claire Holloway lecturing her on lovers' tiffs! And who used a word like *tiff* nowadays, anyway?

"I think I see Caroline Spence," she said quickly. "Maybe I'll just go over—"

"Of course, of course." Claire waved her away. "That's what my parties are for. I like to think mountaineering history is being made in my house every Friday night."

"Right," Susan muttered, making her escape while she had the chance. She hadn't really seen Caroline Spence, but she had seen a break in the crowd around the punch bowl, and she made for it. There were a few debutante types striking poses near the center of the table, but no one she knew. She could get a glass of punch and get out to the deck before anyone even knew she was there.

She was just reaching for one of the crystal punch glasses when a filled one appeared before her. Susan stared at it, trying to put together the pieces. The punch glass. The large, flat hand it rested in. The gold watch with its digital face and confusing array of knobs and dials.

She didn't seem capable of acknowledging his presence, taking the glass, or even making eye contact. She just stood there staring at the filled glass.

He spoke first. "I thought this was what you wanted. Punch."

"Punch," she repeated. Something loosened inside her, and she found herself moving, taking the glass, taking the first sip. It was as sickly sweet as all Claire's punches, but tonight Susan didn't care. She took a second, longer swallow right after the first, hoping the alcohol would calm her.

"Well," she said brightly, wishing she didn't sound so false. "I haven't seen you in days."

"I've been working," Jack said noncommittally.

"So have I," Susan said nervously. "So have I."

"At what?"

The question was such a direct challenge, Susan's head shot up. But there was no hostility in Jack's eyes. His expression was coolly indifferent, as if he were discussing the weather with a stranger he wasn't very interested in getting to know.

Susan was at a loss to how to answer him. If she responded with an equally challenging retort, she'd simply sound hostile. If she answered his question directly, she'd just sound like a fool.

She changed the subject instead. "It's a good thing Claire holds these parties on Fridays," she said. "I'd hate to try to make a training climb with the kind of head even one glass of her punch gives me."

"Really?" Jack asked insolently. "I thought you believed in climbing under any conditions—personal or otherwise."

This time there was no mistaking his intention. He was baiting her. Susan felt the same old flush of anger rising to her face.

"I believe climbing is a sport," she told him icily. "Sport is any activity designed to train the body to its greatest capacity in pursuit of making the seemingly impossible possible."

"Very philosophical." Jack bowed sardonically. "Like most of your philosophy, it doesn't make much sense."

"I've never heard you express any philosophy at all," Susan said coldly. "Perhaps you've never developed one."

There was a quick spark of anger in his eyes. "Quite the contrary." The edge in his voice was as thin and sharp as a razor blade. "I have developed the philosophy of nature at war. We are in an adversarial relation to the elements. We would do well to remember it."

"Really?" Susan drawled. "From what I remember, you were in an adversarial relationship to your crew, not the elements."

"None of them have quit on me yet," Jack retorted. "None of the professionals, at any rate."

Susan couldn't interpret Jack's remark as anything but malicious. He knew just how to get her where she lived, and he had used it. She had every right to want to wring his neck.

"Maybe if you continue the tactics you've been employing so far," she hissed, "they'll mutiny. They're ready to."

There was a sound of shocked, indrawn breath, and Susan wheeled away from Jack to locate its source. She found a circle of half-expectant, half-appalled faces, most of which she recognized vaguely as those of jet-setters rather than climbers. She bit her lip in frustration. Neither she nor Jack had been speaking loudly, but apparently they hadn't been discreet enough. They'd collected a crowd, and it wasn't going to go away until the two of them stopped.

Susan took another gulp of her punch and reached automatically for the ladle in the bowl.

"It's beginning to get a little stuffy in here," she muttered nervously. "If you don't mind, I think I'll go out and get a little air."

Jack's eyebrows rose. "What's the matter? Have you had a little too much punch? Or do you just prefer to leave in the middle of an argument you know you're losing?"

"I'm not losing anything," Susan flared. "I simply

had no idea you were interested in prolonging this discussion."

"I didn't realize we had exhausted our topic," Jack scoffed.

Susan wanted to crush the glass with her bare hands. The room *was* getting stuffy now. There was so much tension in the air around her and Jack she was suffocating in it. And the way Jack was behaving could prolong the agony indefinitely.

Suddenly she couldn't take it anymore. It was more than the strain of trying to conduct herself sensibly under Jack's relentless scrutiny, more than the embarrassment of being watched by a group of people who saw them both as nothing more than actors in a play put on for their amusement. Another, more disturbing emotion was pushing toward the surface.

She'd been aware of Jack's body from the moment he first tried to hand her the glass of punch, but now it intruded on her senses with renewed force. She couldn't explain it to herself, and she didn't want to. It seemed that no matter what happened between her and Jack, no matter what he did to her or she to him, she would always feel this attraction that was stronger and more violent than any set of principles, any mere intellectual theories she had. That attraction had characterized their relationship from the beginning, and now she knew it always would, try as she might to suppress it.

But she couldn't let him see that. Whatever had gone wrong between the time of their last real talk and their last climb together, something had happened that had withered Jack's interest in the relationship they had begun the night he returned from Zürich.

She missed his loving caresses more than she wanted to admit, but she still had her pride. She wasn't going to let him know that, in a very fundamental way, he had broken her. If only for the sake of her self-respect, she would make him think she was as independent and apparently unaffected as he was. But she could already feel the beginnings of the unraveling she feared, and if she wasn't to come apart completely, she had better get out of this room as quickly as possible.

She took one more gulp of her drink and prepared to make her move. Steeling herself, she stared straight into Jack's face, stopped—and almost broke down. Jack's face wasn't hostile now, or cold, or indifferent. It was anxious and caring. She groped futilely for some reason for this change of mood and panicked. She had to get out of here. If she spent one more minute looking into Jack's suddenly inexplicably pleading eyes, she was going to explode.

"I really am feeling a little faint," she mumbled gracelessly as she backed toward the door of the observation deck. "I've got a bit of a headache," she continued.

By then she was at the edge of the circle that had gathered around them, and she turned and bolted, carelessly pushing through the crowd. It seemed an eternity before she felt the cold shaft of wind that told her she was outside, and an eternity longer before she managed to get herself safely hidden in a corner, away from the sprinkling of couples gathered by the railing on the mountain side of the deck.

She clutched the railing next to her and leaned out over it, taking in great gulps of air. Her anger was gone now. In its place was only pain, a pain too wide and deep to comprehend. She had been a fool. She had spent so much time telling herself that she was attracted to the man, that he had a magnetic hold on her, that she had completely blinded herself to the truth. She was in love with Jack Cameron, and probably had been from the first day they met. He was right about that. Love was nothing if it wasn't love at first sight.

It was a realization she would rather not have had. Her love for Jack Cameron was greater than anything she had ever felt before, or anything she was likely to feel again—but there was nothing she could do about it. Even if Jack hadn't been intent on maintaining the hostility between them—and despite that last, confusing look, he did seem intent on it—there would still be the same problems between them. They had already proved to each other that those were insoluble. She couldn't think of anything they hadn't tried; and if they had tried everything, any love they felt for each other was doomed.

She leaned far out over the railing, trying to will the pain away. She didn't think she'd ever stop hurting—or stop dreaming about Jack Cameron. No matter what else happened in her life, he would always be with her. What was she going to do?

She stared down at the lights of the tiny village of Bresson, looking picture-postcard perfect in the clear night air. Then she shook herself and gazed intently at the Hotel Bresson.

She didn't know what she was going to do with the rest of her life, but she knew what she was going to do for the rest of that night.

It was a long walk from the chalet to the Hotel Bresson, and it did her good. Trust the cold mountain air, Susan told herself as she let herself into the ornate lobby of the hotel. The Alps might not cure your pain, but they went a long way toward making you feel capable of facing it.

She hurried up to the desk and rang the bell for the night clerk. Nothing. In fact, there didn't seem to be anyone in the lobby, which was unusual for Bresson on a Friday night in climbing season. All the usual party-goers must be up at Claire's.

Not wanting to wait, Susan made her way to the elevators and pressed the button for the fifth floor. According to Janie's "employee report," which Susan had filled out to satisfy the Swiss Department of Labor, Janie lived in room 521 of the Hotel Bresson.

Room 521 was directly across from the elevator. Susan was relieved to see a light shining under the door. She wasn't sure what she would have done if Janie had been out or asleep.

She knocked sharply on the door, then called out her name when Janie asked who was there. A moment later she heard an elaborate set of bolts and chains being unlocked.

Janie opened the door a crack and stared out at her suspiciously. "What are you doing here?" she demanded. "You're supposed to be at Claire's."

"I *was* at Claire's," Susan said. "I even made nice to Claire. You didn't tell me I had to stay all night."

"That's true," Janie admitted. She leaned out into the hall and peered into Susan's face. "You look terrible," she remarked.

"Maybe I'd look better if I came inside," Susan said. "Do you mind? I mean, I hope I'm not interrupting anything."

"I wish you were," Janie quipped, but she stepped back to let Susan pass. "The room's a bit of a mess. I'm working on our AK reports for the Société des Alpes."

Susan had no idea what an AK report was, and she didn't intend to ask. She swept a bunch of papers off what looked like a comfortable armchair and sat down. Appearances were deceptive. It seemed to be a rock upholstered in velour.

Janie sat on the matching ottoman and propped her

elbows on her knees. "I'd thank you for the visit," she said, "but I have a feeling you have an ulterior motive. You've never been up here before, you know."

"I know," Susan said apologetically. "You spend so much time at the chalet."

"It's got more room," Janie said cheerfully. "What did you want to talk about?"

Susan sighed. Now that she actually had Janie in front of her, it wasn't as easy as she'd thought. What she wanted was a shoulder to cry on, and Janie had seemed like a good candidate. The only candidate, in fact. Unfortunately, Janie's shoulders weren't very soft, and she wasn't making things any easier by giving Susan that bright, expectant look.

Susan rubbed her hands nervously against the slick surface of her gown. "Well," she fumbled, "I know we've been avoiding the subject for days, or at least you have. But if you could just sit still for an hour or so and let me babble, I mean Jack—"

"I knew it!" Janie slapped her hand against her thigh. "I knew you came here to talk about Jack!"

"Well, what did you expect?" Susan asked querulously. "I was at Claire's. And you know how everyone shows up there. And there he was by the punch bowl. And—"

"Don't babble," Janie reproved her. "Not that you ever do anything else when you talk about Jack. Just don't babble *now*."

"I told you," Susan said miserably, "that's what I came here for. I think it might be what I need right now."

"What you need right now is to listen to a few home truths," Janie said shortly. "And if you stay here, I'm going to give them to you."

Susan looked at Janie in surprise. "Home truths?" she asked. "I don't know what you mean."

Janie was in full swing now, on her feet and pacing. "I've been going crazy all week," she declared. "Ever since you came back from that last training climb—or rather, ever since Jack came back, because I saw him first. How you could be such a stupid, pig-headed, unsympathetic daughter of a—"

"Me?" Susan protested. "I admit I didn't quite keep my temper, but it wasn't exactly one-sided, either. Hasn't it occurred to you that we both might have had points in our favor?"

"Not that time," Janie said stoutly. When Susan looked ready to protest again, Janie raised a hand. "I'm not saying Jack Cameron is a saint," she cautioned. "He's got a tendency to deliver lines with a bit more arrogance than he should, and he isn't always tactful. You had every right to clobber him after that stunt he pulled in the dance room. But that training climb!" Janie threw up her hands. "Don't you ever listen to me?" she demanded. "I make friends with cleaning women, with climbers, with shopkeepers, with the chief of police, all to make sure we have all the information about everything we ever need. We finally need the information, I get it, and what do you do with it? Nothing!"

"Janie, what are you talking about?"

"I'm talking about Jack Cameron," Janie said.

"He shows up at our door, and you fall in love with him. And don't bother to contradict me. I *know* you're in love with him. You have been since the beginning. So, good. That's nice for you. I check the guy out, and I like what I hear. I check him out further, and I get hold of a few pieces of information that might be useful to you. But do you use them? Not Susan Elizabeth Reed, girl mountain climber. Oh no! You go right on acting as if everything the man does is directed at you personally. You get out on a face with six other people, and they don't exist. He's picking on *you*."

"You'd have thought he was picking on you, too, if you'd been me!" Susan flared. "I didn't tie this right, I didn't tie that right, I didn't tack his way. And most of it didn't matter, Janie. Not at all."

"And you were the only one he was doing this to?" Janie challenged.

Susan faltered. "Uh, well," she said nervously, "I didn't really pay much attention. A couple of the others were, uh, complaining—"

"It wasn't just you," Janie said emphatically.

Susan flushed. "What difference does it make?" she asked, miserable again. "So he doesn't trust anyone. It isn't just me. He still doesn't trust me. And I can't handle that."

"He trusts you fine," Janie said. "It's mountains he doesn't trust." She stood silently for a moment. Then she sat down on the ottoman again, and when she spoke it was in a softer voice.

"Susan, you've been in the Alps for three years. Jack's been in Nepal for nearly twelve consecutive climbing seasons. You know what climbing communities are like. Everybody knows everybody, and climbers get close to climbers. Nothing terrible has happened to anyone *you* know yet, but Jack . . ." Janie shrugged. "Look at it this way. On the average, three climbers are killed in the Himalayas every year. It's the same in the Alps. The man has a history, Susan. He's made a lot of climbs, and he's known a lot of climbers. At least take a minute to consider the possibility that his mania about safety might have some cause other than distrust of your competence."

Susan sighed. "Even if I knew what caused it, what would I do about it? Knowing how a problem got started doesn't necessarily make it go away."

"It does in this case," Janie said. "I thought the problem here was that you thought he considered you incompetent. If you know that isn't true, couldn't you just put up with his idiosyncrasies? Couldn't you just smile and say 'Yes, Jack' when he starts going crazy? If you have to argue with him, at least wait till he's had a chance to get off the face and unwind. From what Jeanne and Marie tell me, he can't listen to anything when he's actually climbing."

Susan rubbed her face with her hands. She was even more miserable and confused than she'd been when she first started over here, and now she was feeling guilty besides. Why was it that every time she had anything to do with Jack Cameron, nothing in the world made the same kind of sense two moments in a row?

"Why is it I'm beginning to feel everything is all my fault?" she asked Janie ruefully. "I feel like I ought to be wearing a hair shirt."

"Maybe you should," Janie said dryly. "This time."

Chapter 11

EVEN AS SHE opened the door of the chalet, Susan knew she wasn't going to be able to sleep. That Janie had decided to lecture instead of listen was bad enough. The need to talk about Jack and the things that had happened between them was like a tiny hurricane caged in Susan's chest, raging to get out. That Janie had decided to lecture on Susan's *own* guilt and responsibility made it all ten times worse.

Susan had tried to deny it at first, but it hadn't taken her long to realize that Janie had some truth on her side. She *had* been exploding into anger at the merest hint that Jack might not trust her. She hadn't given him a chance to explain when he wanted to. And she certainly hadn't accepted his apologies, when he gave them, with anything even approaching grace. Worse, she had expected Jack to make all the changes and concessions. *He* had to work overtime to cater to her prejudices and appease her fears. She had never even considered doing the same for him. The one time she'd been called on to do so, she'd blown up, questioned his feelings for her, and walked out on him.

She went up to the second floor, slipped down the hall in the opposite direction from her bedroom, and let herself out onto her tiny observation deck. She brushed off one of the white deckchairs that were stacked in a corner—the deck was just big enough to hold two chairs and a tiny table—and sat down in it. At least now she had the night and the cold and the view of her beloved mountains, she consoled herself. She could even see the training face she'd been climbing the day she and Jack met. Seen against the Alps, it looked laughably puny but somehow alive. If she didn't know it was crazy, she would think the face was moving.

She put her feet up on the railing and sighed. The problem with this business of love at first sight, she decided, was that you didn't know the person you loved long enough before the problems started, so you didn't know what to do about the problems. Love, after all, was an emotion that required two very different people to find a way to meld two very different lives into one. It was never easy. Sometimes it was even impossible, though she was beginning to discount her experience with Dan. Her love for Dan had been a childish thing, born of familiarity and false expectations. Her love for Jack was . . .

Was doomed, unless she could think of some way of making the man talk to her. What had happened between the time they talked on the stairs and the time they met on the mountain face for that last training climb? She wouldn't believe he no longer cared for her. She'd seen that look in his eyes tonight. No, something else was going on. She had a terrible feeling that if she didn't figure out what it was soon, she was going to lose Jack forever.

She took her feet off the rail and put her elbows there instead, letting herself gaze absently at the mountain face. It *did* look alive. Well, not alive exactly. Just moving. Undulating upward. Undulating upward very slowly. It was as if—

The realization of what she was seeing nearly knocked the breath out of her. Good Lord! Was the man out of his mind? She leaned farther over the railing to be sure she was seeing what she was seeing. Certainly Jack, who was such a fanatic on mountain safety, would never do anything that stupid. Certainly Jack would never pull a stunt that would make any of hers—or all of them put together—look like a child's game.

He certainly would. The harder she looked, the more positive she was that it was Jack making that training climb. He wasn't inching his way up slowly, either. He seemed to be in an all-fired hurry to get to the outcrop. Susan felt panic wash over her. The damn fool! And he called *her* reckless and crazy! She'd never have the unbounded idiocy to make a face ascent by herself in the dark. When she got hold of him this time, she wasn't just going to kill him, she was going to lock him away in a closet for his own safety!

She tried to calm herself, but even her tense-and-relax exercises didn't work. She tried to tell herself that that could be anyone on the mountain face, that she couldn't make out the man's features and therefore had no way of knowing who he was. But, dammit, no one else in the village of Bresson was that big. That body looked like it covered too much of the face at any one time to be someone else.

She pushed herself away from the railing and began stumbling hurriedly toward the door that led back into the chalet. She was going to find him, she was going to kill him, she was going to lock him up—and most of all, he could listen to *her* lecture on safety for once!

* * *

The face had looked puny from her deck, but it looked large and menacing once she got to the base. Susan stood for a moment, looking up the sheer ascent, trying to make out some definite movement on the face. There he was, nearly at the top. She'd done this climb herself too often not to realize that Jack was now negotiating the most difficult part of it. It was an easy climb, and the stationary pitons should anchor any climber who knew how to use them. But what if Jack was upset, or if he'd had a little too much to drink at Claire's party? Something had to be wrong with him, or he'd never have done anything this dangerous. And if something was wrong with him, he probably wasn't bringing his full concentration to the climb. That would be dangerous under any circumstances.

Suddenly Susan realized she was seeing what Jack must have seen the day they met—the sheer, seven-hundred-and-fifty-foot drop, the litter of sharp rocks at the foot. No wonder he'd been so worried about her. Training climb or not, one false step could kill you.

Janie was right: She'd been a blithering idiot from the first. To think she'd been insisting that Jack's only motivation for lecturing her on safety had been a secret belief that she was incompetent as a climber! He had simply been scared silly that she'd end up killing herself, just as she was afraid for him on the same grounds now.

She didn't dare call out to him. Any sudden unexpected noise could break his concentration completely and put him in even more danger. Instead, she looped her safety rope over the first stationary piton and began to pull herself up. If she could just reach him and link up, everything would be all right. Somehow.

It was a good thing she'd made this climb before, because just as she started a cloud covered the moon and she couldn't see farther than a few inches above her. She knew she was going too slowly, but she didn't dare speed up. She was too confused and jumpy, too likely to make mistakes. Jack had disappeared over the top of the outcrop. Now that she couldn't see him anymore, she felt alone and stranded on the face, an idiot chasing a phantom.

She looped her rope over the second last piton, the one just under the ledge. This was where she had made her mistake the last time, the day Jack had hauled her in. She'd have to remember to be careful. She slipped the toe of her boot into the hold, bounced twice to test it, then slowly swung her other foot up. It caught, and she relaxed. No mistakes this time, she told herself. One more piton and then a swing, and she'd be sitting in Jack's lap.

She looped her rope over the last piton, undid the loop she had just made, made sure her double shank knot was firm, and began pulling.

She remembered what she was supposed to remember just an instant too late. *Don't try the next left hold. It's loose,* she told herself in panic.

And then she fell.

The night wind was much colder than the day wind. That was the first thing she noticed. The second thing she noticed was that she seemed to be developing a positive mania for getting herself into this position on this slope. Here she was again, dangling at the end of a rope tied to a piton seven hundred and fifty feet up the face, without her hat. Why was she always losing her hat?

The third thing she noticed was Jack. He was just where she'd seen him the first time, standing on the ledge with his feet spread apart and his hands on his hips, looking like an optical illusion.

"Don't yell at me!" she called up to him. "Just get me out of here."

"I'll get you out if you answer one question," he called down.

"What?" Susan asked with a slight heart-bounce of trepidation.

"I just want to know if you intend to make a habit of this."

Susan sighed. Somehow it was going to be all right.

"It's not that I don't take these things seriously," she told Jack when he had finally managed to deposit her on the outcrop. "It's just that the fall is so terrifying, that when I realize I'm all right I get so relieved I feel like giggling."

"I feel like spanking you," Jack said, "but since I guess I'm responsible for your being here, I'll refrain."

Susan looked at him curiously. Good heavens, he was handsome. She could spend all day tracing the contours of his broad chest and well-muscled legs. First she'd trace them with her eyes, then with her hands, then with . . . She shook her head to clear it. Two hours ago they'd hardly been speaking to each other, for goodness' sake.

"What are you doing up here?" she asked him. "I thought you didn't approve of making face ascents alone."

"I don't," Jack said. He clucked impatiently. "You're a very affecting woman, Susan Reed. After the way we were at Claire's tonight—"

"The way *you* were," Susan corrected him.

"The way I was," Jack admitted. "I shouldn't have done that, I know, but—Susan, I've been telling myself for the last week that this would never work out, that I would always be bad for you—"

"But you aren't bad for me," Susan said quickly. "You could never be bad for me!"

"I could never stop carping at you either," he said quietly. "I get very tense on a face, and I probably always will. I've seen some very good people get hurt... and worse... and I'm afraid—doubly afraid for you because of my feelings for you, Susan. But if the way I lecture you makes you feel less like a professional, if it saps your confidence, then you shouldn't put up with it. I'd never ask you to."

"But it was partly my fault, too!" Susan wailed. "I've been thinking it over, and talking to Janie Dean. Well, Janie was lecturing me—"

"Was she really?" Jack murmured. "She was lecturing *me* a few days ago."

"What about?" Susan asked curiously.

"About that day in the dance studio." Jack sighed. "About asking the right questions before I start delivering Olympian judgments. She had a point."

"She was lecturing me about learning to put up with your eccentricities on the slope," Susan said. "According to Janie, I should stop acting like a two-year-old with a chip on my shoulder and give in to you sometimes. She has a point there, too."

"Janie always has a point," Jack said with mock solemnity.

"She probably thinks we're hopeless," Susan laughed. "Maybe we *are* hopeless."

"Hopelessly in love," Jack said quietly.

He was standing close beside her now. Susan turned toward him, running her hands over his chest as he clasped his behind her back. It felt so natural, so right, to be standing here like this, feeling both Jack and the mountain air all around her. Then his mouth came down to capture hers, his lips teasing her gently, provocatively.

"I brought a sleeping bag," he whispered. "I was going to camp out until morning, try to think, try to get you out of my system."

"Do you still want to get me out of your system?" Susan asked, shuddering, as his fingers beat a gentle rhythm at the base of her neck.

"I'd rather get you back into my system." He pressed her closer. "It's been much too long."

"Sleeping bag," Susan reminded him as he unzipped her jacket and snaked an exploratory hand under her sweater. When his fingers reached her breasts she gasped, her vague desires flaming into fantasies more distinct, more urgent.

"Right over here," he told her, leading her slowly toward his pack and trying to kiss her at the same time. "It's a very small sleeping bag. We won't have much room to move."

"Something tells me we'll have enough."

They had enough, though for a while their attempts seemed the stuff of slapstick. They slipped off their shoes and jackets, then eased into the bag. Constrained by the bedding, their attempts to undress each other were poignantly comic. Susan was glad of it. The unabated seriousness of their first wild night together was something she'd always cherish, but she liked this gentle, conspiratorial fumbling between them as well. It made her feel they shared much more than passion, that a very essential part of each of them had merged with the other. There would be humor and gentleness between them, as well as desire.

It was only when they lay completely naked beside each other that their true passion flared, and then it was a white-hot heat that swept away everything before it.

Jack's fingers roved restlessly over every inch of Susan's silky skin, and his lips were close behind, trailing a path of fire that ignited every nerve within her. Susan could feel the thundering of his heart as he pressed against her breasts, and the thundering of her own as his hands massaged the sensitive place at the base of her spine.

"Whatever made me think I could give you up?" she gasped. "Whatever made me think I could live for a day without you?"

"I could never give you up," Jack murmured in her ear. "I knew from the day I met you that I could never be without you again. Oh, Susan, I love you."

Then he was on top of her, one large hand tenderly kneading, probing, looking for the spring that would release her deepest passions. He found it. Susan felt a throbbing deep within her, and as the moments passed it grew and grew until she thought it would engulf her. She wound herself around him tightly, feeling the hot pulse of his desire against her flesh. She trailed her hands across his body, reveling in the knowledge that she could excite him as much as he excited her.

"I'm never going to let you get away again," Jack cried hoarsely, clutching her to him. "I'm never going to let you out of my sight, not for a moment."

"I'll never try to leave," Susan promised. "I'll never even want to."

Then he was inside her, and what had been a rhythmic rocking became a wild drumbeat of sensation, getting stronger and stronger until it seemed she would burst into a million pieces before that passionate thunder could become stronger still. Yet it continued, all-consuming, all-embracing, taking her higher and higher into a realm of pleasure and fulfillment so complete and so immediate she was sure nothing else existed in the universe. She and Jack were alone in a night that was forever theirs.

"I love you," he whispered as he plunged into the deepest part of her.

Then the drumbeat became a wave, and she was washed away with it into a turbulent sea of love.

For a long time they lay quietly beside each other, wanting to savor the miracle of what had happened between them. Jack took her hand, and Susan lay against his side, happy just to be near him. They didn't need words to tell each other what they felt, not now. They had said more to each other in their passionate tryst than they would ever be able to articulate.

Then the wind began to blow against them, cold, intruding, sharp. Susan sighed. It seemed like such a pity to move, even to draw the hood over them and shut out the cold. She didn't want to move. She wanted to spend her life in just this position, holding Jack and his love close against her.

"Let's get married," Jack said.

"What?" Susan sat up sharply. The sleeping bag fell away, leaving her naked breasts exposed to the wind. She sat down again and covered herself against the cold. "Let's get married?" she repeated in wonder. "Just like that?"

Jack propped himself up on his side and looked down at her seriously. "Don't you want to?" he asked gravely.

Susan didn't even have to consider it. "Of course I want to," she said softly. "But does it make any sense?"

He cocked a quizzical eyebrow at her. "Do we ever make any sense?"

"No," Susan laughed. "I guess we don't." She paused thoughtfully. "It would be nice to be married to you," she said. "I wouldn't have to wonder where you were. Or worry about your running off after we've had a fight.

You'd always be right where I could get to you."

"I don't think that's the way I'd look at it," Jack said ruefully. "Don't you think we could promise not to fight?"

"Do you think it would do any good?" Susan asked.

"No, but it would prove we had good intentions."

"I have excellent intentions," Susan declared. "How about you?"

Jack leaned forward and planted a kiss on her cheek. "How about this: I promise never to yell at you until I've counted ten, held my breath for at least a minute, and tried to think."

"All right," Susan agreed. "And I promise not to yell at *you* while we're climbing. I'll wait till you're off the face and back in the comfort of your own living room before I let you have it."

"Why do I feel as if you're a lot better at negotiating these things than I am?" Jack mused. "Okay, I'll let it stand the way it is, on one condition."

"Don't tell me," Susan groaned. "You don't want me to climb without a parachute."

"Parachutes would be dangerous on a mountain," Jack chided her. "No, it's the living room I'm worried about. Would you mind very much if I bought us something a little, um, larger to live in?"

"How much larger?"

"A lot larger. Still in Bresson, you understand, so you could keep running the school. But larger."

"If we got something a lot larger," Susan asked suspiciously, "who would clean it?"

"We'll get someone in."

"A maid?" Susan settled back, surprised. Then she wondered why she was so startled. His three books were among the most popular volumes on mountaineering, and they sold consistently year after year. He was probably making a mint. Suddenly a thought occurred to her. "Are you really related to the people who run C & C Sporting Goods?" she asked him. "Do you really refuse to take any money from them?"

He looked honestly startled. "What brought that up?" he asked. Then the light dawned. "Janie Dean!" he hooted. "That woman could give lessons to Interpol."

"Well," Susan said defensively, "you never talk about yourself. If it wasn't for Janie Dean, I wouldn't know any more about you than I could read in your books."

"I take it she has the whole story?" Jack chuckled.

"To hell with the whole story," Susan said. "She even has your blood type."

Jack laughed, hugging Susan to him. "My feeling is that you already know the most important things about me, but let's face it. We have years of talking to do. I'll start when I was just a babe in arms..."

"You'll do it before the wedding, too," Susan told him.

Jack stroked her gently, then swooped to plant a soft kiss under her ear. "I take it it's settled then. We get married. We buy a bigger chalet. We—" He stopped. "Do we climb together or not?"

"I suppose we'll have to," Susan said with a sigh. "After all, there's still the Maidenhorn, and you don't honestly think I'd let someone else partner you on that, do you? Besides, climbing is one of the things I love best. I couldn't bear not to share it with the person I love best."

"I know a lot of things I want to share with the person I love best," Jack murmured, nipping her ear.

Susan felt the tingling start in her again, and she huddled closer to him. "I know how committed you are to this particular course of action," she laughed, "but we can only spend so much time at it, you know."

"Yeah," Jack said. "Just what I was thinking. We can spend *soooo* much time at it."

"That's not what I meant," Susan started to say, but Jack's mouth covered hers, and his arms circled her, and somewhere inside her the pounding had started again.

She gave herself up to the night and the mountains and this man who was offering her more than she would ever be able to fathom.

WONDERFUL ROMANCE NEWS!

Do you know about the exciting SECOND CHANCE AT LOVE/TO HAVE AND TO HOLD newsletter? Are you on our *free* mailing list? If reading all about your favorite authors, getting sneak previews of their latest releases, and being filled in on all the latest happenings and events in the romance world sounds good to you, then you'll love our SECOND CHANCE AT LOVE and TO HAVE AND TO HOLD Romance News.

If you'd like to be added to our mailing list, just fill out the coupon below and send it in...and we'll send you your *free* newsletter every three months — hot off the press.

☐ *Yes, I would like to receive your free SECOND CHANCE AT LOVE/TO HAVE AND TO HOLD newsletter.*

Name _____

Address _____

City _____ **State/Zip** _____

Please return this coupon to:

Berkley Publishing
200 Madison Avenue, New York, New York 10016
Att: Irene Majuk

HERE'S WHAT READERS
ARE SAYING ABOUT

Second Chance at Love ®

"I think your books are great. I love to read them,
as does my family."
— *P. C., Milford, MA**

"Your books are some of the best romances
I've read."
— *M. B., Zeeland, MI**

"SECOND CHANCE AT LOVE is my favorite line
of romance novels."
— *L. B., Springfield, VA**

"I think SECOND CHANCE AT LOVE books are
terrific. I married my 'Second Chance' over
15 years ago. I truly believe love is lovelier
the second time around!"
— *P. P., Houston, TX**

"I enjoy your books tremendously."
— *I. S., Bayonne, NJ**

"I love your books and read them all the time.
Keep them coming—they're just great."
— *G. L., Brookfield, CT**

"SECOND CHANCE AT LOVE books are
definitely the best!"
— *D. P., Wabash, IN**

*Name and address available upon request

Second Chance at Love.